MW01133753

Maggie
Get Your Gun

By Kate Danley

To
Caitlin Bergendahl
Tantris Hernandez
Mary Stancavage &
Tammy Turk

Chapter 1

It was a gorgeous day. A fucking gorgeous day. It was one of those bright, breezy, unicorn-and-puppy mornings. I mean, the unicorns weren't out yet. They tend to be more nocturnal to increase the odds of picking up virgins at nightclubs, but there were a couple pegasi kicking it overhead.

I was in a great mood.

My dad was back.

My mom was occupied now that my dad was back.

And after word had gotten out that The Greatest World Walker of Them All (a.k.a. my dad) had escaped an inter-dimensional prison and saved two worlds from collapse, MacKay & MacKay Tracking was back in business nailing the bad guys and getting paid the big bucks to do it. Nothing like a little hero worship to get the dollars rolling in.

My name is Maggie MacKay. I'm a thirty-something gal. Still single. Probably because these

Irish eyes smile the most when I've got a gun in my hand or a vampire on my stake. Hobbies include punching things. For my day job, I track magical objects and magical beings and put everything back where it belongs. Second in skillz only to my dad, I can travel dimensions between Earth and my home, The Other Side, with just the wiggle of my itty bitty finger.

About a month ago, I learned my dad was trapped in between worlds, so I took down my evil uncle, found a couple Chinese lion statues which were the key to two worlds' survival, and managed to piss off an asshole vampire named Vaclav. But I freed my dad and that's what's important in the end, isn't it? Hugs all around.

It had only been a couple weeks, but the fickle eyeballs of Other Side celebrity had kept their focus on MacKay & MacKay Tracking until just a few days ago. Some illicit affair between a politician and a medusa took over the spotlight, but up until then, the media maelstrom had drummed up some new clients and Frank, the one-eyed ogre who handed out the tracking jobs for the police at the Bureau of Records, seemed to have felt some pressure to give us the higher profile gigs (see: hauling back said politician from an overstayed "conference" in the Mediterranean with said medusa).

Life was good.

I skipped up the stairs to our little office, the sound of my Doc Martens thumping on the linoleum. This probably alerted any bad guys staking out the place I was coming, but, eh, fuck it. I fished around in the pocket of my biker jacket and pulled out the keys to the door.

MacKay & MacKay Tracking Other Side HQ was a small, one room affair over a green grocer shop. Dad started renting it probably twenty years ago and never got around to remodeling. Evidently, the previous owner had a thing for 1940's noir. The two oak desks and matching swivel chairs were old and ratty. A slow ceiling fan and a lame excuse for a window a/c unit tried to keep the summer suns at bay. I loved it.

"Dad?" I called as I pushed the door with my shoulder and flipped on the light. I took my gun out of its holster and walked over to put it in my drawer. There was a note on my desk.

"Taking a vacation day. Your mom says we never go anywhere, so off to anywhere. We'll be back on Monday. Don't dock my pay. I know where you live. -Dad"

I smiled and tucked away the note. I was glad they were getting out. Dad had been trapped in the dimensional boundary for almost two years before I had figured out how to free him. He and

Mom had some lost time to make up for.

Plus, it meant I got the office to myself for a whole day.

The hours passed pretty quick. You know. With a couple snack/solitaire breaks peppered in. The only person I saw was the delivery guy from The Sand Witch Sandwich shop. They made a mean meatball sub and I felt if I was holding down the fort while my partner was playing hooky, the company could afford to buy me lunch.

I tore through an ugly stack of invoicing that had been calling my name from Ye Olde To Do box for awhile now. It sucked, but as they say, those bills weren't going to mail themselves. I mean, they could have, but it is an expensive bit of magic and we weren't there yet.

As the shadows grew long, I put down my pencil and stretched. No bruised knuckles. No trips to the emergency room. All in all, a great day.

I got up to check all the window locks when the door opened. A short, tubby man leaned on his cane, silhouetted by the light from the hall.

I looked at the clock. It just figured. Five minutes till closing.

I sat down as he stepped into the room and gave me a better look at his mug.

He was a wrinkly old gus, bald with a fringe of white hair around his shiny dome. He wore a

white suit and carried a straw hat, looking like he had just stepped out of the pages of Tennessee Williams' greatest hits. Antique looking spectacles perched on the edge of his nose. He walked with a shuffling limp. He was almost as wide as he was tall. If some oompa loompas were around, they could have knocked him over and rolled him out for de-juicing.

"May I help you?" I asked.

"Indeed you may, Ms. MacKay," he replied. He looked around appreciatively, "You have a very nice office."

Politeness always sets me on edge. It's usually a ploy to get someone to lower their guard, which is usually a precursor to someone getting their face ripped off. I decided I should wait to see if this guy was some sort of shape shifting monster beneath the liver spotted wrinkles before I staked him. I motioned to one of the chairs across from my desk.

He plunked himself down with a sigh.

"I just don't seem to move as well as I used to," he confessed. "I'm afraid I would ordinarily have handled this myself, but my get-up-and-go got-up-and-went."

I just stared at him as he giggled to himself, completely oblivious to the fact his joke was for sale in every tourist trap in two worlds and we were dangerously close to after hours on a Friday night.

"You wouldn't happen to have a cup of tea, would you dear?"

The last time some buck called me dear, he walked away a doe, but I bit my tongue and pushed myself back from my desk, "Sure."

"That would be delightful," said the old guy as I walked over to our kitchen, which consisted of a noisy mini-fridge and some wooden milk crates stacked on top of each other. "You know, you sound just like your father."

I plugged in an electric kettle and pulled a dusty Lipton's bag out of the box, "You know my dad?"

"Indeed, he was most helpful on a case several years back."

"I'll have to tell him you stopped by... Mr...?"

"Smith. Isaac Smith," he said, reaching his fat fingers out for a shake.

"Nice to meet you, Mr. Smith," I replied, taking his soft, crepe-like hand in mine. I could tell this guy hadn't gone without a manicure since elementary school. "Sorry to say but my dad's out. You know. It almost being the weekend and all."

Mr. Smith didn't get the hint.

"That is a shame," he said. "I was hoping to speak with him about an employment opportunity.

 6

Perhaps you might be interested."

He had my attention.

"I was recently on Earth visiting some family that still lives there," he explained. "They thought it would be fun to go somewhere almost as old as me, so they took me to Calico Ghost Town. It is on the way to Las Vegas."

I had seen the billboards for the place as I had driven by at 102 miles per hour. I think it was off the same exit as a 1950s diner and a convenience store touting Alien Beef Jerky (I have no idea if it is just a brand name or if they were actually packaging dried up bits of intelligent life for us lower forms to gnaw on). Honestly, if you're driving through the desert on Route 15, you either want to "get to" or "away from" Vegas as quickly as possible.

"Was it everything you had ever hoped for?" I asked.

"And more," he replied with a wink. "We panned for gold and went down into a silver mine. The dry heat was so good for my arthritis. I bought the most cunning little hair comb for my wife, though, and I dropped it somewhere. I'm afraid that travelling back to scour the desert floor is too exhausting for these old bones. I was wondering if I could hire you to find it for me."

"People usually come to me wanting to track

down monsters or relatives, who do sometimes fit into the monster category," I said as I put the tea in front of him and sat down, "Hair combs aren't really my specialty."

"It is an easy task, I assure you. I just need someone able to make the long, out-of-the-way trip for a souvenir this foolish old man paid too much for. I would rather not lose my investment."

Something was fishy. I might be an idiot, but I'm no IDIOT.

"People have been known to kill for trinkets," I replied, thinking of those dumb lion statues that almost took my dad outta the game, trapping him between dimensions for almost two years. "Anything I should know before agreeing to this job?"

"I assure you it is merely a matter of checking with the general store to see if someone returned it to the lost and found. If it isn't there, well, then I'm afraid it will become a much more complicated issue."

"Listen, Mr. Smith, I'm a magical tracker. I can barely find my own keys. If there isn't something magical about it, I'm afraid that I'm about as much help as a four-year old," I said, trying to bait the hook.

He wasn't biting.

"I would like for you to try," he replied, all

doe-eyed and innocent.

The old man stood up and patted his coat pockets. He pulled out a worn business card, the edges soft and creased. He turned the card over and took a pencil from my cup. He wrote a figure on the back of the card before passing it over, "I hope that this will encourage you to consider my offer."

Indeed it did.

I stared at all those zeros for a simple little road trip.

"If it isn't there at the lost and found, I'll give you three hours of searching the area," I said. "And I will charge full price no matter what."

Mr. Smith nodded, "I agree to your terms."

And god help me, because I knew better – we shook on it. Here's hoping I hadn't signed up to be just another corpse dumped in the middle of the desert.

Chapter 2

"Pick up pick up pick up," I muttered, but dad's phone was going straight to voicemail. I sat looking at my cell wondering what I should do. The gig seemed easy enough. Go out, grab the comb, head back, easy money. Easy insane amounts of money. I was a big girl and grown up enough to handle jobs on my own. Still, Monster Scouts taught me to always use the buddy system... especially with skeevy offers that have trouble written all over them.

"Hey Dad," I spoke into the receiver, "Hope you're off having a great time. There's a gig that came in today from an Isaac Smith. Said he's used you in the past for something... Anyhoogle, I'm going to run out to Calico Ghost Town to go pick up a souvenir he dropped and bring it back. Um... I'll call you if I have any trouble. Bye."

I hung up and turned on the engine to my beat up old Honda. Dusk was dangerously close

and I sure didn't want to get caught after sundown. Night on the Other Side had teeth and I liked to be tidily locked away in the hallowed ground of home when the monsters came out for a fast food run. Since my little dustup with the vampire community last month, things had been eerily quiet, but that didn't mean jack squat. I knew they were out there, biding their time. I patted my trusty little neckguard and double checked the lock. It was like a bullet proof vest for my throat. I never left home without it.

I pulled into my driveway just as the sun had tucked itself into bed.

The lights were on in my house.

My stake was in my hand before I turned off my car. Most folks would call the police, but when you're the person the police call when there's an issue... well. A girl has a reputation to maintain.

It didn't look like anyone had forced their way in. The windows were intact, the door was on its hinges, and the roof exactly where it was supposed to be. Check giants, trolls, and ogres off the list.

I crept up the sidewalk, keeping my back towards the wall. Whoever was inside had drawn the shades, which was a fantastic indication that I had myself a bright one. I reached out and jiggled the door handle. It opened with my touch.

 11

"Hello?" came the voice from inside.

Fucking elf.

"KILLIAN!" I shouted, putting my stake back where it belonged, "DID YOU WANT ME TO KILL YOU???"

He was opening up a can of cat food in the kitchen, "Greetings, Maggie. It is delightful to see you, too."

He put the food down in the bowl for my fat orange tabby. Mac was positively smitten with the big blonde lug. Dumb cat.

Killian came over, his merry blue eyes twinkling as he gave me a hug. As he wrapped his arms around me, I felt myself melting into those muscles of solid rock. He was warm and strong and smelled like sage and cedar, but when I realized my thoughts had turned to how nicely I fit against him and how well other things might fit, too, I jabbed him in the chest, "Turn the glamour off, punk."

"You are welcome," he said with a wink.

He's lucky he helped me take down the forces of darkness or I would have staked him where he stood.

For the record, I wouldn't have killed him. Just stabbed him.

Fucking elves.

They live for a whole heck of a lot longer that

12

humans and collect the lady-folk like little kids adopt hamsters. If you don't watch your back, you'll find yourself talked into running around the woods, singing hey-nonny-nonny and braiding flowers in each other's hair until you're old and gray and they look like they just stepped out of GQ magazine.

"How the hell did you get in?" I asked, taking off my boots and throwing my weapons in the basket by the door.

He wiggled his fingers, "Magic!"

I shook my head. I was going to have to boost the security on my place. If an elf can breeze through the perimeter, I was in need of a tune up.

I looked at him, all dolled up in an outfit Robin Hood would have died for. Green tunic, brown boots, and I was pleased to see he had finally decided to give up the tights for a pair of legitimate pants. Okay, so maybe they were a little closer to jeggings, but it was progress.

I gave him a smile, "It's good to see you."

Killian went into the kitchen and brought me a beer. I knew there was a reason I put up with him.

I threw myself onto the couch and propped my feet on the coffee table. Killian sat down beside me.

"So, to what do I owe the honor of this

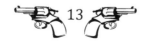

surprise visit?" I asked.

"I was in need of human companionship."

"You're lucky I wasn't in need of human companionship," I remarked. "I could have been bringing home a lucky fella and you would have been in for an uncomfortable surprise."

"I knew there was scarcely a danger of such likelihood," Killian grinned. I punched him in the arm. Wiseass.

"I have missed you, dear Maggie," he said, gripping my hand for a moment. "I have also missed your television set."

"AH! The truth comes out!" I exclaimed, grabbing the remote control.

Killian was a good egg. I had seen him only a couple times since we had taken down the forces of darkness, and I gotta admit, I missed him, too. Sure, he was a pain in the ass and cramped my swinging singles style, but we had gone through a war together and that was enough for a permanent invitation to hang anytime he took a hankering.

I flipped on the TV, "Anything in particular you wanna watch? I think Hovelers has some old crone who's never thrown out an eye of newt…"

"I believe I have seen that one previously," replied Killian, settling in.

I flipped through the channels and stopped

 14

on this one show with ghosts competing to see who can scare a mortal out of a building the fastest. I was rooting for Chuck.

The ghost theme brought to mind my gig for this weekend.

"Ever been to a ghost town?" I asked.

"I try to stay away from that part of the city."

"Not THAT Ghost Town."

The Other Side had a village. It was filled with specters. They couldn't hurt you, but they could scare the bejeezus out of you, and they did, because what else are you going to do if you're dead and bored?

"There's this abandoned mining village outside of Vegas. Some guy wants me to drive out there for this gig and my dad is AWOL. Wanna come?"

"Perhaps..." he replied as we both winced. One of the humans had turned around and rolled her eyes at contestant #2's scare work. That was going to cost some points. "What does it entail?"

"It's a pretty simple open and closed case. We just need to go pick up an antique hair comb."

Killian smiled, "Ah, someone is committing crimes of fashion? I never thought you, of all people, would someday cross that line into the dark realm of smuggling, Maggie."

"NO," I replied. Smuggling is where most

world walkers end up. I, however, was not most world walkers and wasn't about to have my tracking licensed pulled because some fat cat on the Other Side needed a carton of American Spirits. "This old guy stopped by the office, said he worked before with my dad. He lost the comb while he was visiting Earth and just needs us to see if someone dropped it at the lost and found."

"It sounds very easy," said Killian suspiciously. "It is not a trap?"

"It is probably a trap."

"Is it illegal?"

"Do you honestly think I would be involved in something illegal?"

Killian took a little too long getting back to me on that one.

"Come on, Killian. It'll be fun."

He looked at me out of the corner of his eye, "How much will you be recompensing me?"

"Um… isn't the opportunity to hang out in my presence payment enough?"

From the look on his face, I gathered the answer was a negative-on-that-one.

"I'll give you my dad's cut."

Killian grinned and stuck out his hand, "Partners."

Chapter 3

"Killian, put down the pop gun before I pop you one."

Calico Ghost Town is an adorable little institution, a Wild West extravaganza of fun for the whole family.

Unless your partner has never seen a pop gun before and has decided he needs to test out every souvenir in the place.

"But look! The cork goes 'POP' when you slide the handle in and out. It is attached to a string so you can repeatedly pop it. See? Like this! Why, a child could pop the cork all day in the woods without losing it. Like this! See? It pops! Like this! POP!" he beamed as he oh-so-kindly demonstrated... repeatedly... for me.

It was going to be a long day.

Killian had crashed on my couch after a marathon run of terrible television. The wee hours of the morning had come ugly. I woke up

feeling like death warmed over and desperately in need of a caffeine transfusion. He woke up looking like he had swallowed a bucket of sunshine.

We hopped into my car at dawn and crossed the border to Earth via the official portal in Hollywood. We drove towards Nevada and made good time getting to Calico Ghost Town. The highway out that direction is two lanes with almost no exits, so one stupid accident can cause a jam that will ruin your whole weekend. I had hoped to avoid such joys and we had done pretty well.

The town itself is out in the middle of the desert, and the mountains are all sorts of crazy shades of green and red and yellow from all the minerals in the soil. The layers were a geologist's wet dream, folded up from all the earthquakes and tectonic wiggles. According to the signage, the name of the town came from the hills being as colorful as a perty lady's calico skirt. It had an old Boot Hill cemetery and a main street filled with saloons and shops. A couple of busses were parked in the dusty, dirt lot, but the town was big enough to eat up the crowds.

"We're here to pick up a package at the General Store," I reminded Killian, trying to focus my partner.

"...by that slushee popcorn stand?" he asked,

hopefully.

He had already talked me into treating him to a sarsaparilla and a tooled leather wristband.

"Not now, Killian... Afterwards, you can have all the slushees and popcorn you want."

"No, the General Store is by the slushee stand."

I turned around and that fucking elf was right. There it was. In all its adorable glory – the General Store next to a wagon refitted for you to grab some popcorn or some frozen water in your choice of red or blue flavor. I looked over at Killian's smug little face.

"Is that the General Store you were looking for?" he asked, all full of innocence and Boy Scout helpfulness. I could think of a merit badge I'd like to give him.

"Come on. The faster we get this thing, the faster we can leave," I said.

"I am enjoying myself thoroughly. Do not feel you need to curtail this trip on my account. May I borrow $15 to purchase this 'pop gun'?"

It wasn't his account I was worried about.

We walked into the General Store. There were waist-high barrels of candy on the floor and shelves loaded up with old stuff lining the walls. The wood floors were uneven and the beams in the ceiling were covered in desert dirt. The place had never seen a lick of paint and the walls were silver with age. And yes, sure, it was a tourist trap with personalized belt buckles and terrible postcards on one end, but on the other end were cabinets with real things to buy – jewelry boxes and antique purses and hobnail oil lamps.

"Howdy!" I said to the shop lady in period dress behind the counter. Killian wandered in, slurping his slushee as he juggled his new pop gun. I wished him brain freeze.

"We're here to pick up an item for Mr. Smith?" I explained.

The lady's face lit up as she remembered, "Oh, yes! He called earlier to let us know you would be here. We don't get many phone orders."

I tilted my head, "Right... phone orders..."

"I told him we were happy to ship it to him, but he said you were coming out this way for a visit. How nice that you could save him some money on postage!"

Mr. Smith's story about a dumb hair comb for his wife had seemed fishy in the first place. I figured Mr. Smith hadn't dropped the item, but the fact that he had lied to my face about being out here at all... this was getting better and better.

"Lucky for him..." I smiled through gritted teeth.

She pulled out a paper bag with a receipt

stapled to the top, "Here you go! Anything else I can help you with?"

"This'll do me!" I replied.

I opened up the bag and reached inside to get a look at that little hair comb Mr. Smith had been fibbing about. I jerked my hand back like I had been shocked.

Because I had.

"Jesus. What is in this bag?"

The lady's brow got all frowny with worry, "Oh my, did you give yourself a paper cut?"

I realized I was the only one in the room with an inkling of the power in that hair doodad. Ol' Smith had played me. Surprise.

"Yah," I said, "Just a paper cut."

I picked the bag back up and braced myself for the jolt. Fool me once...

"Thank you, again," I repeated as I grabbed Killian by the elbow and steered him quickly out of the store. He looked like he could guess what was going down.

"What is inside of the bag?" he asked.

I picked up our pace and kept pushing him in the general direction of the exit, "Turns out this isn't some comb some poor helpless dude forgot."

"I am shocked," replied Killian drily.

"Funny that you should mention it," I said, holding up the bag, "Because I just was. This sucker is on fire."

Killian shook his head, "What do you propose we do with it?"

"Besides drop it down one of these abandoned mine shafts?"

Killian looked around. A busload of tourists had just unloaded in the parking lot and we were going to have to swim upstream to get to our car.

"Perhaps we could find some secluded location to assess the object?"

"And where do you propose?" I asked.

"The Maggie Mine?" he replied, pointing his finger towards a sign.

There it was. The great silver mine that this whole place built itself around. I had a hole in the ground named after me.

"Fantastic," I muttered.

But silver was good. Silver had a way of insulating magic a bit. So, we hustled over, and much to my surprise, there was a little train station next to the mine entrance. For a few bucks, we could make a loop out into the desert à la antique steam engine. It went out around a stack of white rocks touted as the site of the original mother load before heading back.

I couldn't have asked for a better setting to see what sort of trouble I had gotten us into.

Here's the insider's scoop on dealing with

magic... Silver is one way to foil its dastardly deeds, kind of like rubber insulation around a live wire. But magic has an even harder time working when it is in motion and unable to ground itself. We probably could have looked at the comb in my car, but if you think driving and texting is stupid, try driving and deciphering the mystical properties of a mysterious object.

The train was fantastic.

We climbed aboard a little wooden car hooked up to the red engine. There were other tourists climbing in, too, but it's amazing that if you start coughing without covering your mouth how people naturally seem to pick a cart far away from yours.

The train tooted its whistle and the conductor's voice came over an intercom that seemed to have been constructed by the same folks who make fast food drive-thrus. Killian and I settled in as we chugged away from the station. I wrapped my hand in my shirt tail and pulled out the comb.

It was a brass thing about the size of my palm. Looked a little like a Chinese fan with a couple Egyptian scarabs etched into the spokes. Push the teeth into your Gibson girl up-do and voila! Instant fanciness.

It buzzed quietly as I held it, trying to get

23

grounded.

"It appears pleasant enough," said Killian in a low voice.

"Yah, just like that dinosaur in Jurassic Park that then jumped out to spit poison in that dude's face. This is a shitty little decoration to give to a lady."

"Please permit me to examine it," said Killian.

I poured it into his hand and he began juggling it like a hot potato. Pleasant enough, indeed.

"Give me the bag," he ordered.

I opened it up and he jammed the comb back inside.

"What devilish..." he said as he started sucking on his palm.

"Right???" I replied.

"This is powerful magic. We are in motion and near silver." He shook his head ruefully as he looked down at where it had left a red welt in his skin, "Did it burn you, too?"

"No," I said, looking down at where it had zapped me in the shop. My fingers were tingly but not burned.

"Why not?" Killian asked, little miffed that I wasn't feeling his pain.

"I guess it just likes me better."

Killian narrowed his eyes, "If it likes you

 24

better, perhaps you should wear it."

I socked him in the arm and rolled my eyes as he made an "ow" face, the big baby, "How about we bring it back to our loving patron and see if we can give him a shock?"

Killian stopped rubbing his boo-boo just long enough to oh-so-helpfully point out, "The officials at the portals will not allow you to carry such an object through to the Other Side."

There was a little rule that you had to leave nasty objects on the side that you found them, probably why our Mr. Smith decided to reach out for discrete, professional help.

"Great," I sighed, resting my head in my hands and figuring out why that number had so many zeros on the right hand side. "I mean, I knew better. I KNEW BETTER. But the money was so good..."

Killian nodded his head, sagely, "It was very good money."

"I didn't mean to put us in danger, Killian."

"These things happen."

"I could give back the money," I pointed out.

"You would still have to dispose of the comb responsibly."

I sighed apologetically, "I promise never to take a skeevy offer ever again."

"Yes, you will."

"Okay, I probably will, but I promise never to take a skeevy offer again from THIS guy."

"Shall I hold you to it?"

"No."

"I thought perhaps not."

Our grand loop in the desert was coming to a close and the station was approaching. Our choo-choo came to a stop.

"Listen, we'll head back out to Los Angeles," I said, gathering up my crap so we could get off. "We'll jump through an unofficial portal I know of, which I may or may not have had a part in creating, and we'll call it a day."

"Are you sure?"

A chill ran up and down my spine, "What do you mean?"

"The jade lion caused your father to become trapped in the boundary. Do you know if you can walk between worlds while carrying that comb?"

"Shit."

We unloaded from the car and I tried not to step on any children.

"Ugh, if only I could find someplace safe for it here on Earth while we figured out what it is," I groaned.

"Could your sister guard it?"

"She can barely protect herself against the slobbering affection of that dog of hers. No way

I'm sticking her with this thing," I paused to think, "Are you sure we couldn't just drop it down a mine shaft?"

"I support you in whatever you feel would be appropriate and responsible," Killian replied, darn him.

"All I ever wanted to be was to bring some bad guys to justice. Now I'm stuck running artifacts over the boundaries. I AM BECOMING THE BAD GUY, KILLIAN."

"You are not a bad guy."

"I'm breaking inter-dimensional law."

"You have not broken it yet."

I stared at the bag, "We gotta take it over..."

Killian nodded his head sagely, "If Mr. Smith tracked it down, it is likely that others are looking for it, too."

"Okay," I said. "We cross over and hope I don't get stuck."

Killian gave my arm a squeeze. I was glad to know that if this was my last cross, he would be at my side.

"If you disappear," he said, his soulful eyes looking deep into mine, "May I have your television?"

I hit him.

Chapter 4

We got into my car and pulled out of the parking lot. The road was pretty lousy, filled with rocks and stones. I prayed that I didn't get a puncture. That's all this day needed. And right as we were passing Boot Hill, I heard the hiss.

"Crap."

I pulled my car over and got out. It was flat all right, gashed wide open. I popped my trunk, which appeared to have turned into a second basement while I wasn't looking. I dumped empty shopping bags, clothes, and crossbows on the ground, finally digging my way down to the jack and my spare. Driving on a donut 130 miles to Los Angeles was going to suck. We would have to grab a real tire somewhere between here and there. No way I was getting stuck in the middle of the desert at night with a bad tire. I'd seen that horror movie.

Unfortunately, I hadn't seen THIS horror movie or I would have known to drive on the rim till I got out of dodge.

 28

My first inkling that something was completely fucked up was the sound of stones sliding. I turned around towards Boot Hill. To keep the coyotes from picking the bones of their loved ones, the family members of the dead had stacked rocks above each grave. And the rocks were now shifting.

"Killian!" I warned.

He turned around, "Yes, Maggie? Are you in need of help?"

"Yah, I think I'm going to need a lot of help."

I picked up the tire iron and walked to the cemetery. The vibrations got more violent as I got closer.

The first hand burst through the rubble and pulled himself up. The body had turned into aged, beef jerky out in the desert sun.

"What in Boot Hill did you wake up?" Killian cursed, running over to the pile of crap I had pulled out of the trunk to find some weaponry.

"I don't know," I replied. "I'm just going to start trying to kill it and we'll see."

Two more dried out, dead bodies had pulled themselves out of their graves and were coming towards me. They were fast. They seemed smart. I wacked one guy's head off. He stumbled around, picked it up, put it back on, and came right back at me.

"Not zombies!" I announced, ducking as he swung at me.

I pulled out my stake and chucked it at its heart.

"Not vampires," Killian observed. He had my Louisville Slugger in his hand and started swinging. He was knocking the covers off of these dudes, but they just kept putting themselves back together again. Still, as they wandered around the graveyard looking for their missing pieces, it bought me a little time.

I ran over to my car and pulled out a can of hairspray.

"I do not believe you will be able to style them to death," Killian shouted as he bashed another creature.

Oh good. The elf had picked up sarcasm.

I started the spray as I whipped out a Zippo lighter. With a flick of my fingers, I lit the makeshift flame thrower. The closest monster went up like a roman candle. His charred remains crumbled to the ground. Killian and I stood there for a moment watching him burn.

"Mummies," I observed, "We have mummies. What do you say we start a bonfire?"

"I shall see if the General Store has a stock of marshmallows," Killian replied, turning around to knock down another walking corpse.

 30

I lit them all on fire. Every last one of those bastards.

As we watched them smolder, I could see a park ranger coming over from his ticket stand to see what all the smoke was from.

"Just overheated my engine!" I yelled at him.

"Can I help?" he called.

I so needed him to not come over until these muthas had burned themselves out.

"Yah, could you go grab me some water for the radiator?!"

The park ranger gave me a salute and started jogging up to the town.

I looked at Killian, "We should leave right now."

"I could not agree more."

I looked at my poor car, "And we can't."

Killian joined me to gaze at the flat and all my crap spread out on the side of the road. He sighed, "I could fix it, but you would owe me."

Fucking elves.

"Your own ass is on the line! Don't you think you could skip the favors on this one?"

"It is the way these things work," Killian replied apologetically as he walked over to one of the burning bodies and stoked it like a log in a fireplace.

"Don't I get an employer discount?"

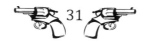

"I am afraid that it is not in our contract."

I looked at the burning corpses. They were already down to the smoldering bones. Fucking magical rules and magical karmic debt.

I went over and kicked one of the bodies. It collapsed upon itself and was nothing but a pile of dust. I shook my head as I muttered, "What made you guys decide you had enough of eternal sleep, huh?"

"Perhaps the comb?" offered Killian.

"I'm thinking that's about the way of things."

I pulled out the baggie from my pocket and leaned up against the stone cemetery wall. Another pile of rocks started to rumble. I stepped back and the rumbling stopped. Stepped forward and it started again. I walked closer to the pile and the mummy came right out. I torched him before he knew what was happening, poor fella.

"Well, guess you gotta get close for the mojo to kick in," I stated.

"Are we going to be raising the dead our entire journey home?"

"Let's hope the mob dropped off their bodies a bit farther off the road."

Killian sighed, "Can you make a portal here?"

I should have said no. There is a reason why portals are carefully mapped out and you don't just go around creating them willy-nilly. You don't

 32

know what's waiting for you through the doorway - could be someplace completely safe and wonderful like George Clooney's boudoir. Could be a vampire lair inside of an erupting volcano. You just don't know. But I really wanted to get home without any more surprises and, stupidly, decided to press my luck.

I reached out into the boundary and gave it a little knick. Salt water gushed in. The good news is that it doused all of the smoldering corpses and pulverized them into dirt, which saved us all sorts of uncomfortable questions from the local authorities, one of which I could see headed my way with a gallon of water right now. The bad news is that closing up the portal made stars dance in front of my eyes. You try pushing back on the weight of the ocean.

"Ugh," I knelt over with my hands on my thighs. My legs were all shaky.

"Are you ill?" Killian asked with concern.

"I could use a soda," I said, trying to ignore the energy drop. "Actually, I might just sit down for a second."

Killian jogged back up to Calico and spoke briefly to the park ranger as I tried not to pass out. He was pointing at me and the ranger was nodding sympathetically before they both trotted off together. I looked down at comb, "You little bastard."

I pulled out my cell phone and dialed The Other Side.

"Mr. Smith speaking."

"I got your comb and we need to talk."

"I am afraid you have the wrong number."

"Listen you old punk..."

"I assure you that you have the wrong number. The person you wish to speak with has an appointment at your office at 5:00PM and I am sure would be quite pleased to meet with you at that time."

I couldn't believe this guy.

"Well," I said, full of piss and vinegar, "I'm afraid I'm stuck and won't be able to make it."

There was a pause on the other end of the line.

"What do you mean 'stuck'?"

"Meaning I've got a flat tire out in the middle of the desert and only a donut to drive on."

Without missing a beat, it seemed Mr. Smith was suddenly all full of helpful solutions, "I could send someone out with a spare..."

"How about sending over someone to transport your little trinket from the gift shop?" I said.

"I am afraid you're the only one able to do that," he replied.

 34

"Ah ha!" I exclaimed, "You KNEW it was magic. You knew and lied to me. What else are you not telling me? Am I going to be able to cross with this thing?"

"You should."

I stared at the phone receiver.

"SHOULD?!?!"

"All indications reflect this should not be an issue."

"You little shit!"

"Contact me when you return."

"Son of a bitch!"

And then the line went dead.

I swore to god that I was going to kill him if the mummies didn't finish me off first.

I jammed my phone into my pocket and lay back down on the ground. I probably should have checked for scorpions or rattlesnakes before flopping anywhere in the desert, but fuck it. I almost hoped a great big old rattlesnake came right over and tried to bite me. I needed something to choke. No, wait. I hoped I got bitten by a rattlesnake and died and Mr. Smith had to figure out some other way to get his precious little comb.

I heard Killian's feet crunching in the dirt. I opened up my eyes and he put the Coke in my hand, "Is everything all right?"

"Yah, just called Mr. Smith and we had a little discussion."

"How did it go?"

"How do you think it went?"

"Shall we concoct your alibi on the drive home or wait until after you're arrested for murder?"

"Any judge in two worlds would consider it justifiable homicide."

"Rest," Killian said, patting my shoulder, "I shall change the tire."

I didn't argue. Killian got the spare on and we were on the road in about twenty minutes. I let him drive. I wasn't feeling like anyone's life should be in my hands anytime soon. The next closest town out in the middle of our corner of nowhere was Barstow. Able to top out our speed at 30MPH, that seventeen mile drive took about forty minutes. As cars whizzed by, tooting their horns and giving us the old one finger salute, I entertained myself with all the different ways I was going to kill Mr. Smith. We finally got a full sized tire at a ridiculously expensive price and were on the road again, hitting Los Angeles about two hours after that.

"Where would you like to cross?" asked Killian.

I would have loved to have just jumped

through one of the lovely legal portals. You know, someplace that would not put my entire career at risk if anyone figured out what I was doing, but I knew too little about the comb. Who knew how many fucking bells and whistles it might set off. I cursed that bastard again for sending me after a stupid piece of jewelry and not warning me that it just happened to raise the dead.

Dad and I had set up an illegal portal out near the San Onofre nuclear plant about an hour south of Los Angeles. The fluctuations of energy made it a little easier to keep things stable, believe it or not. The nuclear signature also hid the entrance from prying eyes that might be looking for a door. There were some smaller portals Dad and I had put together, but none of them were big enough to fit a car.

"Keep heading south," I told Killian.

As soon as you cross the Los Angeles/Orange County line, it is like a different world. The 5 freeway breaks away from urban hell and turns into a really pretty drive. You know. When you're not occupied about getting caught in an inter-dimensional prison. Suddenly, you're out of the city and there's nothing but rolling hills and ocean. I didn't mind so much that this could potentially be one of the last things I ever saw. Sure beats the pants off of some of my other near fatal experiences.   Vampire fights.   Demon attacks. Being left alone with children.

I flipped the switches on the car as we neared the border. The double white globes of the San Onofre nuclear power plant loomed on the horizon like two boobs of death.

Killian looked over at me, "Are you ready, partner?"

"Ready as I'll ever be."

He reached over and placed his hand upon mine, giving it a little squeeze.

And then gunned it as we sailed over the bluff.

Chapter 5

"You fucking bastard."

Mr. Smith was sitting in our Other Side office and he seemed amused by my outrage.

"You agreed that the compensation was fair," he stated, tapping his cane on the floor. "Surely you did not take this job assuming there would be no risk?"

Killian sat in my dad's chair since my dad, mind you, was still unreachable. What a fucking lousy time to unplug from the world.

I leaned forward on my desk, speaking very slowly and clearly so that Mr. Smith understood, "You said that this was a gift for your wife. A trinket. A trifle. A little piece of metal. Instead, I had to use an illegal portal because I was carrying an artifact that wakes every dead thing in a twenty foot radius."

"It doesn't wake every dead thing," that smug son-of-a-bitch pointed out.

"Listen, Killian and I," I jerked my thumb towards my partner, "we were out in the middle of

the desert. We woke up a bunch of mummies. Had to torch them. Blew a tire. It wasn't fun."

"We could have been killed," Killian stated bluntly.

Mr. Smith pulled a stack of money out of his pocket and placed it on the table, "I hope this will ease the discomfort of any troubles you had."

I looked at that pile. It did help. Quite a lot. I looked over at Killian and he gave me a shrug. Sitting up here on my high horse after the grunt work was already done wasn't going to pay the rent, and I sure as hell wasn't chalking this one up to experience. I stacked up the blood money and put it in my drawer.

"The comb, please," Mr. Smith asked, holding out his hand.

I went over to our wall safe and spun the dials. I pulled out the comb and slid it across my desk to Mr. Smith.

He opened up the bag and poured it out into his hand, nodding, "It is quite powerful, isn't it..."

"Why doesn't it zap you?" I asked, a little disappointed he wasn't lighting up like a vampire bat in an electrical transformer.

"I read that this particular comb is powered by the bearer's life force. Channels it into the dead to animate them and such. I'm quite old, so I could never wield it."

"So what you are saying is the more life force you have, the stronger the reaction from the comb?" asked Killian, making sure to look at me as he rubbed where it had burned him good. "One might even say that if the comb gave one a stronger burn, it is because the comb has a stronger affinity... it, one might say, likes that person better than someone who only received a slight shock?"

"I suppose so..." said Mr. Smith, a little puzzled by Killian's questioning.

"I don't think that's what he's saying at all, Killian," I said, cutting Mr. Smith off.

"I believe that is exactly what he is saying, Maggie."

"I think what Mr. Smith is trying to tell us, before you so rudely interrupted him, Killian, is the history of the comb..."

"...and how it is able to magically measure a person's life force, their virility, as it were, which it appears I have in excess..."

"I would be more than happy to surgically remove some of that virility, elf."

Killian held up his hands, "Just clarifying the power of the comb. Please, Mr. Smith, continue."

The old man coughed.

"Please, continue," I said, dragging the daggers I was shooting at Killian back into my

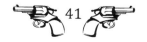

41

eyes.

"Well," Mr. Smith said, shifting in his chair, "it was created for the Empress of China by a powerful sorcerer who based his magic in the Egyptian arts, hence the scarab symbol you can see here."

Killian and I leaned forward as Mr. Smith pointed to the carvings.

"Each line is part of an intricate magical system made for bringing the dead back to life. I believe they act as channels, allowing the energy of the host to flow through them and into the body of the one who has passed. The thing about highly complex magic, though," continued Mr. Smith, "is that it is quite delicate. The form must be preserved. Why, if I were to do something like this..."

He dropped it on the ground, he raised his foot, and crushed it.

"I would render it quite useless."

He picked up the mangled bits and dropped them back into the envelope.

"Your lady friend is gonna be pissed," I said, slack jawed. It takes some balls to go around busting up magical objects. Unless you know exactly what you're doing, the objects oftentimes bite back.

He gave me a slight smile, "I believe she will

be quite pleased."

I shook my head, "Awful lot of work for some mangled metal. Why?"

"I'm afraid if I told you, you would be in quite over your head."

"Listen, I just torched half the heroes of Calico Ghost Town. I think I'm already quite 'in'."

"I was there, too," said Killian as he raised his hand.

Mr. Smith leaned forward and whispered conspiringly, "I am trying to delay the destruction of Earth by gathering up and destroying any magical object that evil might choose to yield."

"Well, shoot," I said. "All you had to do is say so. I'm okay with that sort of life goal."

Killian nodded, "She is. She has saved the world several times."

"Really?" Mr. Smith rubbed his white beard, "Would you like another dip into the ocean?"

"Um..."

"The pay is quite generous and this," said Mr. Smith, holding up the bag, "is merely the tip of the iceberg."

I looked over at Killian but his face was impassively blank. He wasn't going to help me out on this one. Guess he knew I probably wouldn't listen. It's what makes us good partners.

"How big an iceberg? Would it, say, sink the

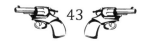

Titanic?" I asked.

"The number of objects that need retrieval make that berg look like an ice cube in a tray," Mr. Smith said, taking out an envelope. He tapped it against his fingers a couple times, almost as if he was sizing me up before he pushed it across the table towards me. "This is the next object on my list."

Killian was giving me just a little shake of his head. It's like we were thinking with the same brain. I managed to stay awake to the end of Titanic and saw what happens when your ego tells you it's a great idea to pit yourself against large frozen masses. I had no desire to reenact any of those scenes, specifically the ones where the main characters died.

I pushed the envelope back, "Listen, Mr. Smith, you seem like your heart is in the right place. But I'm thinking I would like to keep my heart in the right place, too. Namely, inside my chest. I'm going to have to pass on this adventure."

Mr. Smith took the envelope and placed it in my inbox, "Contact me if you should decide otherwise, my dear."

"Well, don't hang around the phone like a mopey thirteen year old, okay? It's been a..." I couldn't quite manage to spit out something like "been a pleasure". So, I just gritted my teeth and

said, "Well... it's been 'business' doing this thing with you."

He put on his old, beat-up fedora and struggled heavily to his feet. The rubber tip of his cane thudded uncomfortably on the ground. Each time it hit, I could hear my mom telling me to be nice to old people, especially old people whose bodies have quit them. I can't believe that I was telling a cripple to go take a leap. But I was. I'm just an asshole like that. An asshole that had a burning desire to see another day.

Mr. Smith held his hand out to me, "I shall be in touch."

"I won't answer the phone."

Mr. Smith smiled, "If experience has shown me anything, you will."

He tipped his hat and walked out.

I looked over at Killian as the door shut, "I'm thinking it might be time to get a receptionist."

Chapter 6

"Hey, Maggie-girl!" called my dad, sauntering into the office and tossing his coat on his desk. His lean, craggy face was burned to that crisp shade of red that only the Irish can do and his shaggy hair was bleached from too much time in the sun. Guess he decided to show Mom that Mediterranean spot we had discovered.

"Productive weekend?" he asked as he sat down.

"Something like that," I said, barely looking up from my disassembled gun. "Nice to see you again."

Dad looked at me and sighed, "All right. What did I do wrong this time?"

"Nothing," I said, shoving the patch and bore brush down the barrel, "Just might have been nice if you had left your phone on."

He slapped his head, "I totally forgot. Sorry about that. International rates are a bitch. Hope there wasn't anything too urgent."

 46

"No, nothing too urgent," I replied.

That's when Dad opened his drawer and saw the stack of money.

"Where did all this come from?" he asked, pulling it out to show me like I wasn't perfectly aware of its presence.

"Oh, yah," I said, maybe just a little smugly, "you might want to check your voicemail."

He put the wad of cash on his desk and felt around his pockets for his forgotten phone. He dialed and punched in some numbers, hung up, then dialed again, then hung up in exasperation, "What's my pass code again?"

"1969."

"Right."

This time he got through. I watched as his eyes got wide.

He covered the receiver, "Isaac Smith was here?"

I nodded and he went back to listening to the message. He sat down in his chair as if his knees were going weak. He hung up and looked at me, all hang dog and guilt, "I am so sorry, Maggie-girl. You should have waited for me."

I rolled my eyes, "It's fine. Killian came out. We had some real laughs, you know, fighting off a horde of reanimated mummies in the middle of the desert sun and all. We got paid. All's-Well-That-

Ends-with-the-Right-People-Dead-and-a-
Paycheck, right?"

"I don't think that's the title of Shakespeare's play, Maggie."

"Are you sure? Because I think I caught it on Masterpiece Theatre. It was either that or Much-Ado-About-Trying-to-Guilt-Your-Daughter-When-It's-Your-Own-Fault-You-Didn't-Check-Your-Phone."

"Listen, I should have picked up. I'll never turn my phone off again. I'll always look to see if I have any messages from here on out."

"Of course you'll turn your phone off and you never check your messages. Now, put the money away and let's get this day started," I said, putting the barrel and spring back into my revolver.

"I never would have let you take a job from that man. You should have held off until you cleared it with me."

I'm pretty sure he didn't mean to make it sound like he was territorially pissing in the proverbial corners of my business-decision-making-skills, but shit, the guy took off for the weekend and left me to make decisions. I had made decisions.

"Listen, Dad. I went out to pick up a lady's comb and ended up having to set a mob of mummies on fire that I accidentally brought back to life. And you weren't here to warn me this dude was on our blacklist. I made a judgment call and earned us a metric shitton of money, so you're welcome. In fact, I think you owe me a raise."

"Maggie, Isaac is the one who sent me after the lion statues," he said. "He told me he had purchased the lion online and just needed someone to pick it up. Sound familiar?"

So Isaac was a sneaky little bugger and had gotten us both... Like father, like daughter.

"Don't take any more jobs from him. Leave those jobs to me," Dad said in a voice that sounded like he was in no mood to be trifled with.

Except trifling is what I do best. I gave him a look, "How about neither of us take any more jobs from him, huh?"

"Maggie..."

"Because he offered me an open ended gig," I said, tossing him the envelope Mr. Smith had left, "and even though I told him no, now I'm thinking maybe I should reconsider."

He caught it midair, opened up his desk drawer, threw the envelope in, and slammed it closed.

"I mean it, Maggie."

"Whatever."

"I have worked for that man and if he comes here again, you kick him out. You call me. You do

49

not speak to him until you clear it with me. Do you understand me, young lady?"

"You're not the boss of me."

"Margaret Gertrude Mary MacKay!"

I couldn't believe he was so mad he used my full name.

I put the slide back onto my gun, "Fine."

"Fine."

We sat glaring at each other for a minute.

"Did you have a good vacation?" I spat.

"It was great," he growled.

And thus began another Monday at MacKay & MacKay Tracking.

Chapter 7

I flipped through a folder in my inbox. Teach me to run downstairs to pick up a soda. Work magically shows up on your desk.

"Did you put this in here, Dad?"

He was scrolling through something that appeared utterly fascinating on his computer, "Yah, I mistakenly thought you were going to have a quiet Friday, so I swung by Frank's this morning to get us some jobs. He specifically picked that peach for you."

"Really, Dad? You're pawning this off on me?" I groaned as I read through the pages. The case involved a genie and a missing necklace.

Genies fall under the category of "dimensional demons". They don't belong on the Other Side. They come from a third plane, which most folks just refer to as The Dark Dimension and leave it at that. The Dark Dimension houses about all the delights you'd expect from a spot with such a cheerful name.

 51

Genies can be called to both Earth and The Other Side by summoning circles and incantations, just like a regular demon. The difference is that genies can be bound to bottles and toted around, which is why some dumbasses think it is a super awesome idea to have a genie as their very own special, wish granting pet. What the books don't tell you is that once your three wishes are done, you are genie jam-on-toast. Genies have lives and families in The Dark Dimension and they tend to get a little cranky when they can't make it home in time to watch their favorite game shows. They fucking hate granting wishes. And since you aren't their master anymore, they take a certain delight in making sure you viscerally understand that sticking them in a bottle was not the way to go.

Also, genies are just jerks.

This case did not look particularly nasty, but dealing with genies is never nice.

"Come on, you're not sending me out on this alone."

Dad held up another file that was about five inches thick, "I'm afraid I have to go deal with this one. You want to trade?"

I shook my head as I looked at his pile, "What did you do to piss Frank off this time?"

"He's not a particularly chatty fellow, is he?"

"Shit, Dad, did you try talking to him? NEVER

try to talk to him."

"I forgot."

"You have been away for way too long..." I looked at my case, "So my guy is wanted for lifting some jewels that didn't belong to him... wait. Are these magical jewels?"

"No."

"I've heard that one before."

"Frank said they were plain, old, ordinary rocks out of the soil."

I looked over at Dad and groaned, "You know I'm no good at that sort of thing."

"You gotta learn sooner or later how to track down ordinary objects, Maggie-girl."

"That's why I keep you around."

"Head on out," he said, standing up and stretching. "I'll get my job done, you get your job done, and I'll meet you back here for lunch."

I was two seconds late shouting, "Not it!"

Dad grinned and pointed at me, "You're buying."

Chapter 8

The street was bustling. It felt good to get out of the office.

The Other Side grew and developed over the years, just like Earth. There are parts of town that have retained the charm of those eras gone by. This particular spot was home to a lot of Studebakers and outdoor cafes. The entire place looked like 1940's New York. Some of the local monsters even went so far as to fade their hides to grayscale. The rest actually had gray scales.

The report said the jewels were stolen from a locked safety deposit box from right under the nose of a rich ol' witch, so I headed over to the scene of the crime. She lived in the penthouse at the top of a schwanky hotel, so I grabbed the elevator going up, and knocked on her double door.

"Come in!" called the distressed dame's voice.

I pushed the brass handles and walked in. The walls were white, the thick pile carpet was

white, her silk peignoir that she somehow thought was appropriate to wear at noon was white. The only color in the room was her painted, ruby red lips and ebony hair set in tight pin curls.

"Miss Veronica Dubois?" I said, hand outstretched as I walked over. "I'm Maggie MacKay."

She stared in horror at her carpet. Guess her lily white rug didn't like the underside of my ass-kicking boots.

"Sorry," I said. "I'm sure you've got someone you can pay to get that shampooed."

"Who are you?" she asked with a long look down her short, pug-like nose.

"The police sent me. Heard you had a necklace lifted by someone magic-like. When that happens, the po-po call me to dig around in the dirt."

I flopped down on her couch as she looked at me like I was something that crawled out from the shower drain, which is actually a problem on The Other Side.

"Listen, I promise not to get your couch dirty," I said as I rubbed my palms on her cushions to prove I had washed my hands.

Miss Dubois blinked towards me and looked like she was going to hock something up. Judging from her dress size, it was probably the Tic-Tac she ate for breakfast. On a plate. With a knife and fork. I imagined she probably dabbed her mouth with a napkin when she was done.

"It's fine," she said, biting off her words. "I'll just throw it out after you leave."

"Or you could... clean it..."

"That's not the way I choose to live my life."

"Right," I said. The place was so posh, she probably blew her nose on dollar bills and dried her dishes with twenties. "So, this necklace, what can you tell me about it?"

"My grandmother's necklace," she whispered, suddenly over the outrage that I was sucking up air. After a dramatic pause, she got up and wrung her hands like we were on a fucking episode of Dynasty. She waved an arm to a portrait over her mantle and then bit her finger, "She entrusted it to me on her deathbed and now it is gone! Gone! I am ruined!"

The gal in the painting was a lovely Asian woman in traditional dress. Her hair was set with combs, which, frankly, I was feeling like I had my fair share of over the weekend. Around her neck was a necklace of rough, yellow stone.

"Is that the necklace?" I asked, pointing at the pretty dead lady.

"Indeed. It has been passed down through the generations until finally it came to me and now

I have lost it."

"How did you lose it?"

She waved me over to another picture frame, which was hanging off its hinges. The door to the safe behind it was open.

"He," she said, pausing to make sure I caught every word, "took it."

She flopped down on a chair and buried her head in her arms, "As I slept, he broke into my home and took it."

"Who is 'he'?"

"I already told this to the police."

I barely controlled the eye roll wanting to spring itself instinctively in my sockets, "I admit I might not be the foremost expert in translating subtle emotional cues, but I sense that recalling this theft is a little distressing for you. I promise you only have to tell your story one more time and that time is to me. Right now."

Miss Dubois sighed, dragging her head up as if the mere task was of Herculean proportions. If I didn't know my dad would give me lip all day for mouthing off at a client, I would have been happy to put things in perspective for her.

"I was in my washroom, powdering my nose..."

"What kind of powder?" I asked, pulling out my pen. There are so many substances that can attract a genie, many of them powder-like.

She looked at me like I was an idiot, "Let me rephrase that in a way that someone vulgar like you might understand. I was 'taking a piss'."

"Well why didn't you just say so?" I replied.

"Are you sure you're here to help?" she asked.

"I promise I'm really good at this."

"I'm afraid my confidence in your abilities is flagging," she said, her face looking like she had smelled something unpleasant. I sniffed my pits.

She got up and walked over to her bedroom door to re-enact the moment for me, I think just in case I was too dumb to follow the narrative, "I heard a noise and came out of my room. I looked over at the safe and there was this... it was a man... except he was almost stone like... except like a cloud... well, you know what genies look like."

And I do. They look exactly as she described.

"So," she said, "I threw my shoe at him and he disappeared before it hit."

"Shoe?" I asked, making sure I heard that right.

She took off a feathered mule, "They're made of silver and the heel can be used as a stake. If you press this jewel, it ejects a stream of either holy water or salt. Despite the judgment I see in your eyes, I am a witch. I'm not completely helpless."

I gave a low whistle, "You totally just won points in my book. Let me see that. I'm thinking mama might need a brand new pair when she gets this case wrapped."

She held the shoe away, "You couldn't afford them."

So much for points.

"Right," I replied drily, "so he grabbed the necklace and was gone?"

"The end."

"Was there anything special about this necklace?"

"No, it was just a bunch of rocks that my grandmother brought with her from Earth. I don't even know why my family thought I should be the guardian of her necklace, but they said it was important and that I would be cut off if anything ever happened to it," she waved her hands at her penthouse, "I need you to find that necklace. I need you to get it back for me before I am turned into a homeless beggar on the streets."

"Well, if you ever decide to pawn those to make rent," I said, pointing at her fancy footwear, "I wear a size nine, too."

Chapter 9

A gremlin in a newsy cap was hawking the headline from his stack of papers. A trolley car rumbled by filled with devils in zoot suits. A pair of cthulhu were holding tentacles and gazing into one another's eyes, not paying any attention to their chocolate éclairs. It had to be true love. I'd been to that café and they make a fucking awesome éclair.

Distracted by dessert and dreams of creamy injected goodness, I didn't notice the gorilla until he had knocked me over and grabbed the file out of my hand.

Yes, a gorilla. I mean, not a real gorilla. It looked like one, but my tracker senses were a-tingle, because that ape was no ape. It was some sort of shape-shifter in a monkey suit. I watched him lope down the street from my sideways view on the concrete. People were staring. There was no way I could let him go without a fight, not if Dad and I expected to make rent next month. Other

Siders look for weakness. They will fucking eat you up if they figure out they can do it. And the gremlin newsboy was actually starting to drool. Guess if there weren't enough stories in his paper, he wasn't above setting the gears in motion to get the next day's scoop.

I rolled off of the sidewalk and took off in a full sprint. I passed an alleyway and caught a glimpse out of the corner of my eye of someone ripping out the pages of my file and dumping them on the ground.

The gorilla wasn't a gorilla anymore.

In non-camouflage form, I'd bet cash money it was the genie I was trying to track down. This guy... well, it wasn't really a guy. Genies don't have dingle berries so it was more of an "it" with masculine features. It was smooth and deep, dark blue as midnight, other than its knife-like pearly whites and beady little red eyes. Instead of legs, it floated on a cloud of smoke. And it was pissed.

I turned to the side and pulled my stake out of the top of my boot.

"Ripping up the pages won't help," I said. "We totally made copies."

The genie hissed and its fingers morphed into claws.

"Where is it?" it breathed, shaking the file at me.

"Where is what?"

Porcupine spikes sprouted out of its shoulders.

"I know a great esthetician that can wax that for you," I offered.

"I asked you, Maggie MacKay, where is it?"

"I'm so overjoyed I don't have to go tracking you down to hell's half-acre, I'm not going to bother asking how you know my name..."

"Your name is not important!"

"...but I will take the time to mention, you crazy, shape shifting, genie dude, that I have no idea what you're talking about."

It gave me a growl and I crouched into a defensive posture, waiting for that fucker to spring.

"I should kill you now," it stated.

"You do that, and I won't be able to tell you where whatever-it-is you're looking for is."

It hissed in frustration.

This was definitely not one of the brighter bulbs on the tree.

"The necklace, you stupid human. Where is the necklace?"

That took me off guard, "Necklace? They told me YOU had it."

"I DO NOT HAVE IT! TELL ME WHERE IT IS!"

"I have no idea! That's why I'm trying to

track you down!"

"YOU LIE!"

"Your mom lies."

"Do not trifle with me!"

"Do you see my nose growing? I'm telling you the truth."

"TELL ME WHERE IT IS!"

"I don't know, you dumb demon. I do know that shouting at me isn't going to help me find it any faster. If you would just shut up for a second, maybe we can figure out what's going on."

It roared in anger, but clapped its trap and resorted to just glaring at me.

I held up my hands, "I was told by a witch that you stole the necklace..."

"It was not there when I opened the safe," it hissed.

"You expect me to believe someone came along and stole it just moments before poor little powerless you showed up? Tell me another. What did you do with it?"

The genie hung its head, it seemed almost in shame. You know, if evil had shame. Usually, they're pretty unapologetic jerks.

"I came to take the necklace to my dimension..." it said.

"Dude, that's a long way for a bunch of rocks on a string."

The genie started laughing, which, trust me, is not a sound you need to hear.

"Is that what they told you?" the genie drew closer. It started circling me, "Each bead contains the power to control one soul. Thirty-three souls held in thrall by thirty-three brimstone beads."

What was it with people feeling I shouldn't be privy to vital information like... oh say... that the thing I was tracking down had freakin' scary powers? First the comb. Now the necklace. Mr. Smith I could understand. The man was clearly a psychopath. But my own father? He said that according to Frank, this was just a piece of bad costume jewelry. Unless the police weren't aware that the necklace was anything special. Which would mean the witch lied... or that she wasn't aware of what she had... but this genie knew what it was and what it did...

I started circling him back, "Brimstone? You mean sulfur? That is one stinky necklace..."

"Brimstone does not 'stink'," corrected the genie.

"That's like wrapping thirty-three rotten eggs around your neck. Who would do that to themselves? For thirty-three souls? Totally not worth it."

"How many souls do you possess, Tracker Maggie?"

I stopped, "Um... one."

"Then do not look down upon the means for such control."

I started circling again, "Seriously, you can keep the necklace."

"DO NOT JEST!" the genie roared.

"Okay, okay, don't get your magic exhaust cloud in a bunch. Let's recap. There is a stinky necklace..."

"It is not 'stinky'..."

"Which was stolen..."

"...I do not know how..."

"By someone."

"That is correct."

"Before you could get there."

"Yes."

"Except we have a witness," I pointed out. "The lady of the house caught you red-handed. You broke in and were standing in front of her empty safe."

"She discovered me at the precise moment I discovered the necklace was not in the vault. I have been tracking this necklace for over a century and someone---"

"---got to it before you did," we said in unison.

You know you've got an issue when you're sharing the same brain with a genie.

I looked that genie dead in the eyes and said, "I don't believe you, but I don't not believe you, either."

"You will soon see that what I say is true," it snarled.

"What do you exactly want this necklace for?"

"The necklace was created to bind an army of my kind to the wearer," it growled.

My brain started rattling through the damage that thirty-three genies could do, "That would suck."

"The three wish rule does not protect us. We are forced to stay, enslaved to the stones, doing their bidding with no hope of freedom until the necklace is removed. But no longer! I have followed its trail for over a century! The necklace must be returned to The Dark Dimension and destroyed!"

I twirled my stake in my hand as I thought. I didn't trust this genie as far as I could throw him. And he was big and heavy and I could not have thrown him very far. But he was an enemy of my enemy...

I pointed my stake at him, "Okay, here's the deal. I'll look for your necklace. But if I find it, I destroy it. Meanwhile, you broke into someone's house, so you have to turn yourself in. And pony up some restitution to that stuck up witch."

66

"Never!" it hissed.

"Come on, don't choose the hard way..."

I hated when they choose the hard way.

"I shall walk to the ends of the earth, scorching the ground and destroying all that stands in my way until I find the necklace!" it bellowed with the fury of a Category 5 hurricane.

I rolled my eyes, "No, you won't."

"NO ONE CAN STOP ME!" it screamed.

"About that..." I pointed down at the ground, "While we were circling one another, I decided to drop a salt circle on your ass. Sorry about that."

The genie looked down and roared. I pulled out a plastic bag of Morton's Kosher from my waistband and pulled the rubber tube out of my pants.

"Yah, I just ran it down my leg. When I figured out you were going to be a jerk about all this, I unclipped the clothespin and, voila! No hands!"

"YOU CAN'T DO THIS TO ME!"

"Sorry, you're having a rough day. What can I say? When it rains, it pours."

He beat on the boundary of the salt circle with both fists, crying, "NOOO!!!"

"Come on, you big baby. It's not that bad," I pulled out a bottle from my jacket pocket. It was standard Other Side issue, designed specifically by the Other Side police authority for detaining genies. I broke the seal and unscrewed the lid, "This, however, is gonna suck. By the authority invoked upon me by the Magical State of The Other Side, get inside the bottle, you dumb lug."

Chapter 10

I dropped the bottle off at the police station. My friend Lacy, the blue gal who works in intake, was unfortunately off. She and I have a streamlined system worked out for when I have a "person of interest" who needs processing.

Instead, there was an eager new guy covering the desk, which meant by the time I had gotten through dotting all the "i"s in the genie's paperwork, it was mid-afternoon. The cops weren't too happy that I didn't have the necklace, but grudgingly thanked me for at least hauling in their man. I pinkie swore I'd locate the necklace the first chance I got.

But I wasn't going to track down jack shit for anyone until I got some food in my belly. My stomach was growling like I had a bunch of cave trolls living in there. I opened up the office door, subs in hand, and shouted, "Dad! I'm back."

His desk was just as he left it. Guess his job was taking longer than he figured. I threw one sandwich on his side and flung myself into my

chair, opening up the wrapper and sinking my teeth into all that goodness.

The light was blinking on my messages and I turned on the speaker phone.

"Maggie MacKay," came a stilted Chinese voice I only knew too well. The sandwich caught in my throat. "You come now. Your father bring werewolves to my house. You come NOW."

It was Xiaoming, this cranky Asian dude who lived in Chinatown. He might have helped me track down my dad and also maybe disposed of a magical artifact for me that would have destroyed several worlds. I probably owed him.

The thing is, he also had eerie magical powers and controlled two concrete, guardian lions statues that came to life whenever he was in trouble, so I knew it had to be bad.

I grabbed the phone and hit redial. It rang a couple times and Xiaoming picked up the line.

"Xiaoming? It's Maggie. What's..."

"Where you been? It been three hours!"

"Sorry, I was taking down a genie..."

"You stop making excuses! Your father come here looking for vampire information. Werewolves find him. They wake my lions."

A little seed of panic rose in my belly, "Where's my dad, Xiaoming? Put him on the line."

"He gone now."

70

"WHAT? Where?"

"He gone. You come now."

"Where did he go, Xiaoming?"

The line went dead. He hung up on me.

I rested my head in my hands and then picked up the receiver. I pounded Dad's number into the phone. He didn't pick up. Like always. I tried again. Straight to voice mail. I ended up leaving him three messages but knew he had probably already forgotten his pass code.

I got up and paced around the office. I knew what I had to do, but man, a girl shouldn't have to make those sorts of calls twice in one lifetime. I would have gladly faced a horde of vampires at this moment rather than pick up the phone. But I knew I didn't have a choice. I pulled together all my courage and dialed the number.

"Hello, Mom? I think I lost Dad again..."

Chapter 11

I finally made the jump from The Other Side to Earth after a stupid long wait in line to get through the one official portal that could actually fit my car. It dumped me out on Mulholland, right above the Hollywood Bowl, which is convenient to nothing. Rush hour in Los Angeles was in full force and the freeway from Hollywood to downtown was bumper-to-bumper. Everyone and their mother was between me and where I needed to go.

I finally pulled in front of Xiaoming's place in Chinatown and checked my watch. He was going to be so cranky...

I got out, marched up his sun-baked steps, and knocked on his flimsy metal screen door. Xiaoming's concrete lions were looking a little worse for wear. They were displaying some new cracks and their nails looked like they could use a good manicure.

"Sorry, guys," I apologized. "I have no idea

what is going on."

The lions gave me the silent treatment.

Xiaoming shuffled over in his ratty old robe and open-toed terry slippers and undid the door. He grunted at me from behind the long ash of his cigarette. His entire apartment smelled of old fry oil, stale smoke, and chrysanthemum tea. I followed him through the beaded curtain into the kitchen and sat down at the table.

Mom had been terrifyingly quiet on the phone with me. I knew I wouldn't be getting any presents from Santa if I didn't find Dad and get him home before the street lights came on.

"What happened to my dad?" I asked.

Xiaoming pointed at a folder I had seen my dad looking through earlier. I picked it up and flipped through. There, on the top page, was a crime sheet on a certain dude named "Vaclav".

My dad had decided to start hunting down Vaclav and not tell me about it.

Vaclav was the head of the vampires. The Big Bad. Vaclav wanted to take over Earth and celebrate with a champagne pyramid, except instead of champagne, it would be the blood of every man, woman, and child on the planet.

He and I were not friends.

He and my dad were not friends.

And, despite the fact my dad and I had agreed

that we weren't going to take any more jobs from the old man, behind the crime sheet was Mr. Smith's envelope, the one he had given to me when he mentioned he'd like to keep some choice magical artifacts out of the hands of the bad guys.

This led me to believe that Vaclav and Mr. Smith were not friends, either.

And it looked like my dad had decided to let Vaclav know he wasn't going to be getting any love letters from our crew.

"Shit."

"You not a lady. You swear too much."

"Xiaoming, I swear just the right amount," I said, "Tell me what happened."

"Your father come looking for information on a vampire. Says man needs him to find jade comb. Only your father bring werewolves with him to my house. They fight."

"Werewolves need a full moon, Xiaoming."

"You know nothing. Why you so stupid? They just need moon in sky. It there right now. You look up sometime, then you not say dumb things."

I could think of a lot of dumb things I wanted to say in that moment, but I figured I should find out what happened to my dad first.

"Okay, Xiaoming, my dad came here looking for a comb..."

74

"Your father show me that envelope and said old man Mr. Smith need comb to fight vampires."

So my hunch was right. Mr. Smith was behind this latest dust-up. I was going to have to get him a trophy to let him know he had made the Top 10 on my shit list.

"So what did you tell him?" I asked.

"I tell him jade comb belong to Empress."

Xiaoming glared at me over the table as if this was all the information a person could possibly need to go find out why werewolves had attacked in broad daylight and why dads disappeared.

"Dude, you've got to give me a little more to work on."

Xiaoming shook his head like I was a disappointment to my ancestors, which I probably was.

"How you not know about jade comb? You world walkers in America are so stupid. You not even read your own history?"

"I sucked at reading, Xiaoming. It's why I punch things."

Xiaoming sat back and took a long drag off his cigarette, settling in to tell what I was sure to be a fascinating tale.

"It brought to America by washer woman working on railroad," he began, "With jade comb, you can jump cities. She get comb in China, jump,

jump, she is in San Francisco."

This guy was ridiculous. What he was saying was impossible.

"Xiaoming, I have been jumping dimensions since I was old enough to wear a training bra. You can't jump locations in the same world."

"You can with jade comb. Dimensions like hair of beautiful concubine. Comb wraps worlds around its teeth and you can jump one teeth to next teeth. Same world, threaded through comb."

So, here's how the whole dimension jumping thing works. Imagine each dimension is a sheet of paper and you have a ream of it in your hands. As a world walker, I'm like a hole puncher and can poke a hole in any piece of paper and go up or down to the pages above or below. But you can't jump in the same dimension. You can walk (or drive or bus or whatever) from one end of the paper to the next. But in order to jump in the same world, you'd have to fold the whole ream of paper in half and bore holes through every piece of paper to get to the other side of the one you're on.

What Xiaoming was saying is that this comb could take a single sheet and fold it like a fan. Then, you could punch through the fold and get to a different spot on the same page. If this comb could do what he said it could do... and the vampires got it first... I believe the proper phrase is "a world of hurt".

"Where was this comb last seen, Xiaoming?" I asked.

"I do not know. She hid it. But washerwoman work in silver mining town called Calico. Her tub now is a place for stupid tourists to stand next to and take dumb picture for online photo album."

Two magical hair accessories in one week and it wasn't even prom. And it was all going down in Calico. Something was up.

"Wait, Xiaoming," I said holding up my hands. "I was just there. We picked up a brass comb..."

"Brass comb to make army. Jade comb to transport army. Quartz comb to protect army from silver weapons..."

"THERE IS ANOTHER FUCKING COMB?!?!"

"...and necklace to control army."

"Wait... necklace?"

"It is very stinky. It is made of brimstone. It smells like gassy old man eating old eggs. It all supposed to make the Empress invincible. She is not good woman. But washerwoman stole combs from her and came to America to hide them. She hide in railroad camps, but Empress came after her. So she went to place with silver in the ground. Empress's tracker could not find her there. Too much silver."

The pieces all started to put themselves

together.

"Wait, I just was talking to someone on The Other Side who owned a stinky necklace. She said it was just stolen."

"Empress necklace has been stolen from washerwoman's granddaughter?" yelled Xiaoming. He let loose on a string of expletives that I'm sure would have been jarring to even my delicate ears if I spoke Cantonese. I breathed deep as he paused long enough to light up another smoke.

"I'll get it back, dude," I said, holding up my palms to try and get him to chill the fuck out. "The police have me on the case. I'm tracking it down. I already got the genie who was after it."

Xiaoming exhaled an angry plume, "Hopefully genie stole it and will take it to The Dark Dimension where belong. That magic never supposed to be on Earth. That is why washerwoman granddaughter was supposed to keep it safe on Other Side. She shames her family."

"I'll make sure to pass that along to her," I said. "Listen, hopefully this is all nothing. My dad is probably off picking up the jade comb or the quartz comb or whatever and I'll get the necklace and that will be that."

Xiaoming picked a tobacco leaf off his tongue and wiped it on the tablecloth before continuing, "He bring werewolves to my apartment."

"Sorry about that," I said, not quite sure what he expected me to do. "I'm glad you weren't bitten."

"My lions are best protectors in China. They would not let stupid werewolf bite me."

"Well, that's great," I said, trying to figure out how to get this conversation back on the track of where my dad might be, "So, the werewolves came and they fought and then my dad...?"

"Poof! He gone."

"That doesn't help a whole lot, Xiaoming. Poof? Was he injured? Did he say where he was going?"

"He fine. My lions fight werewolves. He leave. They leave. Now, you leave. Go find combs and hide them. Get Empress necklace back and give it to washerwoman's granddaughter or to genie."

"How about I find my dad and make sure he's okay first, Xiaoming..." I offered.

"This is your fault. You must make better."

"This is totally NOT my fault."

"I help you and your father and you bring werewolves to my house and make lions angry. You get the combs and necklace of Empress."

"How about YOU get the combs and necklace of Empress, Xiaoming."

"I am portal to China. If I leave, portal will

collapse."

"Xiaoming, you are full of moo shu pork."

"You know so much about portal to China, wise guy? You not even know how to jump in same world. You going to tell me how it works?" he glared at me.

I pointed out, "You left your apartment just a few weeks ago to haul Killian and I out of Chinatown on your silver handcart. You can leave just fine."

"That different."

"You head out to play poker with my priest, Father Killarney, on a regular basis."

"I am on schedule now."

"Oh, so you're suddenly on some sort of important portal schedule?"

"It my shift. If I leave, portal to China will collapse."

I wasn't going to argue with him, it was a losing battle, "Okay, Xiaoming, I'll find the fucking combs. AND the necklace. Where would you suggest I begin?"

"Where washerwoman hid them."

"Xiaoming, she hid those combs over a hundred years ago."

"Then you start looking now, lazy."

Chapter 12

There was no way I'd get all the way out to Calico before nightfall just to see if I could catch some 100-year old magical trail which may or may not be there. Besides, after the little incident with the mummies, I felt the need for backup before I went driving out into the middle of nowhere to track down a "harmless" hair ornament. Just as I was getting into my car, though, my phone rang. It was Dad.

"WHERE THE FUCK ARE YOU!?!?" I shouted at the receiver.

"I'm fine, Maggie-girl!" he said. "I'm fine. There's no reception in the desert."

He sounded like he was talking into a tin can, but I still heard the edge in his voice.

I closed my door and locked it.

"What's going on, Dad?"

"Listen, there is a second comb…"

"I know. And a third comb. I just left Xiaoming's place," I said, looking up at our cranky

friend's apartment. "Just to clarify our earlier conversation, I thought we weren't ever going to work with Mr. Smith ever again, which is funny, because you left your folder and it happened to have Mr. Smith's job in there."

"After you left to track down that genie, Maggie, I opened up the envelope and realized what it was. The vampires are trying to assemble the Empress's Set."

"Yah, Xiaoming got me up to speed."

"Did you get the necklace?"

"No," I replied. "I caught the guy, but he didn't have it."

My dad let loose with a tirade of expletives. I held the phone away from my ear until he wound down.

"God, Dad, you sound just like Xiaoming."

"We hit it off."

"Listen, I'll find the necklace. I'll find the third comb. It's gonna be okay. Where are you?"

"I'm leaving Randsburg," he said.

"I don't even know where that is."

"Don't worry about it. It's got an old silver mine. Mr. Smith said in his envelope the jade comb would be there and it was."

"Well... good job, Dad. Sorry you had to fight some werewolves. Um... do you want me to pick up a pizza... or something...?"

I had no idea what you're supposed to say to someone who you thought might have been ripped apart by vicious monsters and then turns out to not only be just fine but also managed to secure a really important artifact in his downtime.

"Listen, Maggie, I'm taking the comb to Ghost Town tonight."

"Whoa whoa whoa whoa WHOA. Ghost Town? Not 'a ghost town' but 'The Ghost Town'?"

"Did I stutter?"

"Why in cuss would you think that was a good idea?" I asked.

"Mr. Smith said so."

"And if Mr. Smith told you to jump off a bridge, you'd think that was a good idea, too?"

"You think bringing this mess home is a better idea? You wanna explain to your mother why a pack of werewolves ate her hibiscus?"

I looked up at Xiaoming's apartment. Mom sure as hell didn't need us to bring something ugly back from the office. I should have listened to that pesky little voice in my head that knew Mr. Smith was trouble. I KNEW he was. If I had just told him MacKay & MacKay Tracking was closed for the weekend, we'd all be kicking back watching reruns instead of making runs out to the desert...

I think Dad took my silence as ire instead of introspection, because he sounded like he was trying to smooth things over, "Listen, there's a lot of silver in the ground out there in Ghost Town and a bunch of poltergeists to guard it. If dumping things in the desert is good enough for the mob, it is good enough for us, right Maggie-girl?"

"Why can't Mr. Smith just destroy it?" I asked, feeling like this whole drama could be over with a hammer and a couple of whacks.

"Who knows? But I've picked up several items for him over the years and he's always had me drop them off in Ghost Town. It's an easy game. Probably where he keeps his secret lair. I'm betting it's safer than hiding it in a hole in his backyard."

I couldn't believe my dad, "You never bothered to mention to me that you were making regular trips out there because...?"

"Why? You hate Ghost Town."

"Touché."

"Listen, in the envelope was the info on the quartz comb, too, Maggie. I put it in the safe. Can you track it down? Meet me out in Ghost Town? I'll show you all my old haunts."

"Nyuck, nyuck, funny guy."

There are big, tough football linebackers out there who are afraid of spiders. And I might be able to stake a vampire with my eyes closed and one arm tied behind my back, but ghosts? Man.

They were my kryptonite.

"I'm not setting foot in that place, Dad."

He was saying something, but the line started crackling.

"You there, Dad?"

"I'm here, Maggie! Listen, tell your mom I'm fine. I'll be in Ghost Town. Find the other comb!"

And then the line went dead.

I stowed my phone in my purse and started my car.

Fucking Ghost Town.

Chapter 13

I leaned my head on the kitchen counter thinking about how the day had gone from bad to worse. I had swung by the office on the way home and picked up the quartz comb file. Seems that, indeed, I had another long ass haul to Calico ahead of me. My poor old car was going to need new tires before all this fun was done. If there was such thing as a frequent drivers program, I'd be halfway to a free road trip. I had called Killian on my way back to my place and expected him any time.

I opened up my freezer and the thought of nuking dinner was too overwhelming. I poured some milk in a bowl and grabbed a cereal box. True to Murphy's Law, there was a knock at the door. I looked sadly down at my crispy "O"s, which were now gonna get all soggy, but set them on the counter. I wiped a drip of milk off my lip and opened up the door.

"Greetings, Tracker Maggie!" squeaked a familiar little voice.

"Pipistrelle!" I smiled. I loved that fucking brownie. He had taken a job keeping my sister's house clean and protected. From what I heard, she was living like a queen.

"How did you get over here?" I asked, ushering him in.

He wiped his bitty feet on my doormat and jumped over the threshold like a kindergartener playing in puddles.

"I am here on official business!" said Pipistrelle, his little chest all puffed up. He held out a lavender envelope glued to a lacy doily.

"Thanks, Pipistrelle."

I took the envelope and opened it up with my finger. It was a gold embossed invitation to dinner Wednesday night from my twin sister, Mindy. Her husband, Austin, was out of town, and she had mentioned a couple days ago she might have the family over. I just hadn't thought I'd need to rent a ball gown. I mean, my sister could give Martha Stewart a run for her money, but this was a little over the top even for her.

"Mindy could have just... called..." I started, looking over at the brownie.

"I told her I would invite you!" said Pipistrelle.

The pieces were all starting to fall into place. I guess there are only so many tubs a brownie can scrub before you start inventing projects. Or start saying "yes" to projects he's invented.

"Ohhhh..." I said. "Well, you little knee high messenger, you tell her that I would be greatly pleased to join her Wednesday night, especially since you made it so fancy. Did you want me to fill out this RSVP card?"

I held it up and Pipistrelle shook his head from side to side, "I will remember!"

"I'm glad to see you're taking such good care of my sister."

Pipistrelle beamed and then seemed to remember something.

"This note was on your car," he squeaked, waving a little white piece of paper, "I thought I should give it to you before something ate it."

I took the folded piece of paper, "Good thinking."

I opened it up and read, "*We know you seek the combs. Bring them to me or Isaac Smith will die. –Vaclav.*"

And then the paper lit itself on fire.

Fuck.

Chapter 14

"Hey, Killian!   Thanks for coming over so late."

I scanned the outside and it seemed fairly free of monsters.   A couple of witches were walking their hobgoblins, but nothing out of the ordinary.   Killian stepped through the door and gave me a full body hug.

"This wasn't a booty call," I said, pushing him off my leg.

"An elf should be allowed his dreams," he sighed before giving me a wink and going to the kitchen to rummage through my refrigerator. "If you did not contact me for the pleasure of my company, to what do I owe thanks for this summons?"

I leaned against the doorway, "Wannna save the world again?"

"Any particular reason why we should save it at this particular moment?"

"Remember that can of worms you and I

 89

pushed to the back of the pantry? Well, Dad decided to open it. We're mixed up in some fun with Mr. Smith. Again."

I handed him the growing folder of the stuff I'd gotten from both Xiaoming's pad and the wall safe. Killian grabbed the whole jug of orange juice. Guess he figured he probably was gonna need a drink after this. He picked up the folder and started thumbing his way through, his eyes getting bigger with each passing page.

I summarized recent events for him as he read, "Dad was attacked by some werewolves over at Xiaoming's place because of some jade comb that went with that brass comb we brought over. So, he has that comb and is headed out to Ghost Town to get rid of it. I have to go pick up a matching quartz comb and meet him there. Somewhere along the line I also have to find a necklace that can trap souls. I'd handle it myself, except Vaclav left me a lovely little note on the windshield of my car saying he was going to kill Mr. Smith, which I'd give to you to read, except it spontaneously combusted."

Killian walked into the living room and took a big long swig.

"So, I need to find a comb, get it to my dad, and try not to get my client killed by Vaclav. You in?"

Killian looked down at the file, "Killing Mr. Smith... we are positive this is undesirable?"

Chapter 15

"Is it too late to renegotiate the terms of this engagement?" asked Killian as a scorpion scuttled across our path.

"Come on. It's just a little desert critter," I said.

"I prefer woodland creatures."

"Like what?"

"Bears and wolves."

I elbowed him in the ribs, "Who knew a big guy like you was scared of an itty bitty bug?"

"Who knew a mortal like you was afraid of ghosts."

"That was a secret I told you in confidence, elf."

It was early afternoon. We were a little later getting started than I would have liked, but traffic between Los Angeles and Calico had decided to make us its bitch. Fortunately, the sun was still pretty high in the sky and Mr. Smith had included a

treasure map in his "Welcome to Your New Gig" Info Packet. We had parked out by a bunch of RVs and campers and followed the hiking trails, which skirted Calico proper.

We were on the far side of this great big hill, which was a part of the Silver King Mine. Evidently it was like a honeycomb inside with something like thirty-miles worth of warren-like tunnels. The paperwork said Mr. Smith thought the hairpiece was in the old Glory Hole, the great big pit that made boys into men and fortunes were won. No, not the town's cat house. The Glory Hole, home of the muthalode.

There was a tiny little doorway in the side of the mountain. The rocks were black with all the silver, almost $2 million still left in the soil, according to the "Fun Facts" list. I gave a low whistle, "We could make a killing with all this ore."

"Indeed, we could become very wealthy."

"I meant we could kill a bunch of monsters with it, Killian."

"That, too."

I pointed at the gully we'd have to walk through in order to get down to the entrance, "The good news is that the silver ore should make traveling through this path uncomfortable enough to keep away any magical creatures."

"As long as they have not found the quartz

comb yet..."

"Yes, as long as they have not found the quartz comb yet, party pooper. We should get moving before they beat us to it, unless there are some more of my hopes you'd like to dash. Shall we?" I asked, putting on my spelunking hat.

Killian swept his arm, "After you."

"I don't think that's particularly the chivalrous thing to do in this case."

"I am sure it is."

"I think you should go before me," I said as we started down the side of the embankment, rocks sliding beneath our shoes.

"I am here only in a backup capacity."

We went in together.

I flipped on my headlamp and flashed my light deep into the tunnel. It appeared we were alone. I hated that neither of us would put "crawling through dark places" on our Top 10 List of Awesome Things. Someone needed to be the spunky cheerleader on this adventure. I looked at Killian, "I wish you were a mountain dwarf."

"The feeling is mutual."

I tried to soothe myself with the notion that as soon as we nabbed the hair doodad, we could get the hell out. I reached out with my senses to get a lock on the comb, but I couldn't feel it. I hoped to god that it was just all this silver masking its whereabouts and not that we had been A) beaten to it or B) lied to.

Other than a couple spots that had seen some fantastic little cave-ins, the passageway was tall enough for us to walk down, minding our feet didn't trip over the ore cart tracks. Last thing either of us needed when crawling through an abandoned mine that we weren't supposed to be in was a sprained ankle.

It's hard to tell the passage of time when your whole world exists about twenty feet in front of you and you've forgotten your watch. It seemed like we were walking forever.

"Listen, I always look at the clock on my cell phone," I explained. "I just didn't think to remember that 4G coverage probably didn't extend down into the bowels of the earth. What's your excuse?"

"My sundial does not work underground."

That's when my little magical radar pinged.

"I got a lock on it, Killian."

The call felt like it was coming from the "left" and "below us", so I turned us at the next intersection.

I stopped Killian, "Did you hear something?"

He got really tense, "Like what?"

"Just sounded like a rock..." I reached out my tracker senses and didn't feel anything. "Probably just gravity collapsing the place on our heads. Come on."

The path dead ended into a drop. And I could feel the comb was absolutely in a you're- going-to-have-to-climb-down-this-shit direction.

"Crap," I said as I pulled a rope and some wires out of my bag, "Looks like I've gotta go below decks."

Killian placed his hand on my shoulder, "Maggie, I cannot allow you to proceed alone."

I looked up at him and grinned. He actually looked worried. The goofball really did care.

"Listen, I'll be fine," I said, handing him my pack, "Watch my shit and make sure I can get back up. It'd suck pretty bad to get stuck inside a hill for eternity because of one lousy job neither of us wanted."

"How important is this object?" Killian asked.

I set the line and stepped into my harness, "Important enough to strap a rope around my waist and lower myself into a hole."

He looked like he might want to hug me for good luck, so before he went turning this mission into some awkwardly mushy moment, I jumped over the edge.

I rappelled down the side, trying to keep things going at a controlled rate. My feet finally touched the ground.

"I hit bottom!" I called up.

Distantly, I heard Killian reply, "I shall await your return!"

So, my sister Mindy and I used to play this game. She would hide Mom's tarot cards and I'd sniff them out like a bloodhound. You know, with less floppy ears and drool. My sister might fight you on the drool.

Technically, this should have been just like that game, except that the area of play was considerably larger and the whole place was enshrouded by silver, which caused all sorts of weird echoes. It didn't mask the magic all together. I could feel the comb was somewhere, but it created these weird pings every time I sent out my bat radar.

I pulled out my wooden stake, figuring I needed something to ground myself with. The sterling one my sister got engraved for me at Things Remembered would definitely have been overkill. It was a little like dowsing for water, except I was the old dude walking around with a piece of wood pointed at the ground.

It worked, though, because what seemed like only twelve years later, I reached the glory hole. The cavern was so big, my weenie little light barely pierced the darkness. I listened for any sound of monsters creeping around, but didn't hear anything.

Which is unfortunate, because someone happened to be home. The second I popped into the hole, it came flying at my head, trying to knock out my light. I lifted my arm to block the blur of motion headed towards me.

It was a vampire.

It's always fucking vampires.

He tried to hold my arm to bite it, but I swept his leg and he dropped like a sack of potatoes. He didn't give me any time to gloat because he was up on his feet again. He stepped outside the perimeter of my light.

"Marco..." I called.

"Polo!" he cried as he tried to jump at me from behind.

I flipped him over my head and raised my stake to nail him, but he was gone.

"Marco..." I called.

"Polo!" he screamed as he came at me again. He tried to pin my arms at my side and I could feel his fangs scraping along my neckguard. I backed him against the wall and started slamming him into the stone, again and again and again until he let go. I turned to stake him, but he had disappeared.

"Come on, dude. It'll just be one little poke and you'll go right to sleep," I explained, getting

my silver stake in my other hand.

"Why do you invade our den?" the vampire hissed.

Great. Mr. Smith had directed us to a vampire den. I suddenly understood why the comb had not been retrieved before. I knew one old man who was not going to be having a good day once I got out of this.

"Just antique hunting..." I replied, trying to spot him.

The vampire came at me and all I managed to do was stab his arm. He roared, but I knew I hadn't done any damage.

"Are you one of Vaclav's minions?" he screamed at me.

"Ew. Dude. No. I hate that guy."

"You lie!" he roared as he came at me again.

I could tell from his voice where he was coming from and I had my stake braced and ready when he rushed me. It got him clean through the sternum.

He looked down at it, as if in shock, "It was supposed... to... protect me..."

And he slid to the ground. And wouldn't you know it, he was wearing a purdy lil' quartz comb right in his purdy little hair. I took the comb off and cursed as it zapped me.

"OW! Muther fucker. You'd think I'd learn," I

said as I dropped it in my pocket.

I leaned my elbows on my knees and looked at the vampire. He looked angrier than a cat who fell in a bathtub.

"Listen, it only protects you against silver. This stake is wood." I removed the wooden stake and slammed him through the heart with the silver stake. "This one's silver. Feel the difference?"

He gasped and died.

I wiped both stakes off on my legs and holstered them up before gingerly taking out the comb.

The translucent stone face was carved almost exactly like the brass one we had found. It even had the same scarabs etched into the surface. It looked like something a Spanish señorita might wear in her hair, draped with a lace cloth. It was certainly lovely, if you overlooked the fact a bunch of monsters were hoping to make it next season's fashion trend.

I swung the light on my hat around the glory hole looking for the exit. The cavern was filled with so much treasure, it looked like something straight out of a pirate movie.

I was tempted to shove as many goodies in my pocket as I could carry, but I knew it'd turn into that whole monkey-with-a-banana-in-a-cookie-jar-who-dies-because-he-didn't-let-go-

before-the-monsters-showed-up thing. The vampires were gonna be pissed someone had found their secret hideout. And I didn't want to be around for them to figure out it was me.

I took off in a sprint, totally creeped out that my entire life depended upon one little light bulb attached to a helmet. Without it, I'd be lost, but with it, I was practically ringing the vampire dinner bell that lunch was served. I reached the end of the tunnel and the cliff face leading to Killian. I tugged on the rope.

"Is this elevator going up?" I called.

"Are you safe?" asked Killian.

"Safe, but I would prefer if I could take the express to the top."

I attached the rope to my waist and started the climb. Fortunately, the miners hadn't seen a reason to polish the walls to a high gloss shine, so it wasn't too tough going. And it felt like Killian was gonna haul me all the way up if I gave him half a chance.

Finally, I reached the lip of the upper path and Killian's hand was there to catch me. I bent over at the waist and rested my hands on my thighs.

"Fuck, I am out of shape," I said, wiping the sweat from my brow.

"Did you find the object?" asked Killian.

101

I pulled the comb out of my pocket and held it up for him. Killian shone the light upon it and nodded, "That is a comb."

"It is zapping me good, so I know we got the right one." I grabbed my bag and hooked my head towards the direction of out, "We need to go."

"Any trouble?"

"Yep," I replied.

We both broke into a trot.

"What happened?"

"Vampires."

"How many?"

"Just one."

"That is not unmanageable."

"There are more."

"That is problematic."

We broke into a run.

"Oh, and this comb doesn't seem to need life force, because it worked really well for the vampire," I said.

"Such an object would make a vampire fairly powerful," remarked Killian.

"Yep."

"His clan would most likely be extremely interested in regaining it."

"Yep."

We doubled our pace.

The sky was totally dark by the time we

got out.

"How long were we down there?!?" I groaned.

"Let us continue this conversation while we travel, Maggie," Killian urged.

The moon was really bright and the sky was clear. I guess it was nice that we'd at least get to see what was attacking us. I flipped off my headlight as we walked. Killian did the same.

"This was fun," I said. "We should come hiking here again."

I cut off my words midsentence. A shadow was moving. I took Killian's hand and dragged him behind a rock. Killian looked at me with concern. I pointed at the hills. The shadow moved again, but this time it was a little closer. Killian became as still as a cat, watching the vampire as he picked his way down the hill.

Killian grabbed my wrist. He didn't need to ask me twice. We ran along the gully, then up the slope of the dry riverbed.

We popped out in the far end of historic Calico. There was an old school in front of us. We sprinted to the door and I rattled the handle. It was locked. I froze as another shadow moved on the other side of the school. I pushed Killian down behind the white wooden steps, and we crouched, trying hard not to breathe as footsteps passed by so flipping close. I had no idea why the vampires hadn't smelled us yet. All I could guess was that the silver ore was dulling their senses, which then made me wonder if there was such thing as silver perfume because that'd be awesome to walk around with an invisible cloak of unsniffability.

The first vampire was now in the wash. The one by the school house slid down the hill and met him, and then a third guy came in off the historic Main Street. They huddled together like an offensive team figuring out the next play and then broke to march towards the mine. If we had been just a few minutes later, we would have been trapped in that hill like prairie dogs in game of Wack-a-Mole.

"Interesting," Killian whispered. "How many more vampires do you believe are below?"

"One is too many. I should not have to worry about vampires out in the middle of the desert," I hissed. "How did the sun not bake them?"

"The vampires must have been hiding underground in the old mines since last nightfall. Are you armed?"

"Does a cow have teeth? Of course I'm armed."

I pulled out my silver stake and my wood stake. I was armed. Just not heavily armed.

"One stake for each of us…" Killian said.

I watched the vampires disappear into the

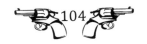

hillside. A thought popped into my brain, "I wonder whose side they are on..."

"I believe 'not ours'," said Killian.

"The vampire I killed in the mine had a grudge against Vaclav. Makes me wonder if they are locals or intruders..."

"Hopefully, these are intruders and the other vampires living in the tunnels will keep them occupied."

We needed to get to the car. Or find a threshold where we could hide out until morning. We couldn't risk going door-to-door along the main street. There was nothing but museums and shops, which the park rangers would have locked for the night. I looked up.

When the miners came to Calico, they actually built apartments into the hills. They were little more than some rocks and boards beneath some outcroppings. Crude, sure, but serviceable. They had doors and iron barred windows and did I mention doors?

"Killian! Think we can reach that one?" I asked, pointing to one of the sturdier looking dwellings. It was sort of on the way to the car and looked like it could give us some cover until things settled down.

He gave me a nod and we made a dash through the sagebrush. Killian stepped lightly, his fairy feet barely touching the ground as we picked our way up the narrow, dirt path. But my big, fat, noisy human feet slid on the gravel and knocked a couple stones down the hill.

A vampire jumped out right in front of us.

He licked his fangs.

"Are you a good vampire or a bad vampire?" I asked.

"Master Vaclav sends his greetings, Tracker Maggie."

"Bad vampire. Got it."

The vampire hissed, "Give me the comb."

"I'm sorry, I am fresh out of combs," I replied.

"You lie, Ms. MacKay."

"Really, we just want to go home," I replied. "It's late. Tell your master I have no interest in combs. As soon as I find it, I'll make sure to know how he can find my listing on eBay."

"You shall not leave here with a Comb of the Empress on your person!"

"Come on, dude. I'm tired and cranky. Don't make me kill you."

The vampire laughed, "My master will be most pleased when I tell him I have recovered the comb AND destroyed you."

"I hate setting someone up for a world of disappointments, but I'm afraid I'm going to have to break your heart. Try recovering this, jackwad!"

Now, I have this thing I do. My dad dubbed it "The Maggie Move" the first time he saw me pull it off. If I hadn't gone into tracking, I seriously would have pursued a career in professional baseball. I take my stake and I can throw it right through the heart of a vampire. Dad and I even went down to the batting cages once and clocked my pitch at 90mph. It is killer. It hits those vampires right in the strike zone and they go down. Done and done.

But I was standing on a gravelly, rocky outcropping in the middle of the night with a great big heavy backpack on my back. I was a little off balance and just as I was about to let that vampire have it, I stepped on one of those rocks wrong. My ankle turned and I felt something pop.

The vampire was on me in a second. I flung him to the side and he rolled down the hill. Killian caught me under the arm and we ran. Okay, I limped and Killian hauled me along as he ran.

The vampire launched himself into the air and landed in front of us. Killian blasted him with some energy thing from his hand. It flung the vampire one hundred feet to the side.

"Hey! I thought you couldn't do magic without someone owing you?"

"That was for me."

"Glad I could glom on."

"We could pretend you owed me, though."

"Don't push it, buddy."

We made it inside the apartment and I slammed the door closed behind us. The vampire flung himself against it and the windows, but the iron bars held the threshold.

I slid down to the ground and rubbed my ankle. Damned rock.

"Maggie, we cannot allow him to leave here alive," said Killian.

"Killian, I can't fight with this dumb ankle," I said. It was turning a horrible shade of purple and was already swelling up. Any old witch doctor on the Other Side could have pointed their finger and healed me on the spot. Unfortunately, I only had an elf. "Can you zap me and make it better?"

"I have long dreamed of having an opportunity to 'zap' you, Maggie," Killian said, sounding like a man interrupted just before he could bite into a hot Kobi burger, "But the healing magic to fix you requires a boon, and unfortunately, if I died before it was collected, the boon would pass along to my victor."

Meaning if something got Killian, I'd owe a favor to a vampire. And taking a wild guess, it wouldn't have been half as much fun.

"I could not place you at such a risk..." he said as he nailed me with his baby blues, clearly trying to figure out how big a risk it actually was.

"Take the risk!" hissed the vampire from the window.

"Shut up!" Killian and I shouted back.

Fucking vampires.

"Give me your stake," Killian said, holding out his hand.

"Come on, Killian, I can't let you go out there," I replied, trying to talk him down, "Can't you just blast him from here with that self-preservation magic you just fired off?"

"It was a prepared spell I had constructed. I do not have another."

"Oh, the mighty elf has no more magic. He is trapped with his whore and is scared like a baby," the vampire taunted, and then started mumbling a little song and dance about how we were stuck in a hole and he was going to kill us. Great. Death by dinner theater. It was a new strategy but surprisingly effective.

"I'm shocked this didn't have a Broadway run," I said as the vampire finished up a verse with something that looked dangerously close to jazz hands.

Killian shook his head, "If I had held off a few moments longer to allow him to come closer, my magic might have inflicted some damage…"

"Listen, everyone has prematurely blown up a spell before they meant to. It's perfectly normal."

"Do not make me feed you to the vampire, Maggie."

"We'll wait him out until morning. This'll be fun!" I said, pointed at a rusty bed post and a broken chair that were there in the hovel with us. "I'll be like a slumber party. A very, uncomfortable slumber party. With vampires."

"If we wait any longer, he will tell his master he found us."

"Don't use logic with me, Killian."

"You know I am speaking truth."

"He is! I shall tell my master! I shall tell my master all about the little mousies I have caught!" the vampire shouted.

I looked at Killian and sighed. I was beat and this pain in the ass vampire needed killing. I pulled out my stake and handed it to him, "Don't get yourself dead."

He nodded.

"And take this," I said. I spun the locks on my neckguard.

"I cannot..." Killian started.

I took it off and rubbed the scars a vampire had once given me when I had tried to fight without protection, "I'm going to have a tough enough time taking down one bloodsucker, let alone two if he turns you. Consider it an investment in my own long term survival."

Killian took it from me and clicked it into place. He gave me a nod and took a deep breath.

"Hey! Vampire! Is that Vaclav?" I said, pointing off at the horizon.

Sure enough, our little thespian looked over to see if the biggest director of vampire drama was catching this act.

Killian had sucker punched him before the guy even had a chance to figure out I'm an excellent liar.

I heard the sound of scuffling and roars of anger. I pulled myself up, clawing my fingertips along the side of the wall. I propped my elbows on the window ledge and peered out.

Killian and the vampire were scrapping on the ground, the vampire trying to hold the stake away from his heart and push it into Killian's chest. The vampire's skin hissed every time it hit the ground. Too bad about that silver allergy. Still, Killian had his work cut out for him just trying to stay alive. It was a down and dirty street brawl. The elf wasn't half bad. You know. For an elf.

But Killian got him. He flipped the vampire over and nailed him through his back. I was impressed. Score one for the living.

Killian turned and looked at me, standing over the vampire's corpse with the stake in his hand. He was all wild and manly and sweating and

out of breath with the moonlight spilling on him. Under different circumstances, a girl might have been talked into playing a round of some Texas Hold 'Em. Git along little doggie.

Killian grinned, I'm pretty sure reading my tells like a champion poker player, but he just came in, swung his head under my arm and said, "Come on, Maggie. We should get to the car before something eats us."

The reminder that we had some baddies out there waiting to rip our throats out and only one neckguard between us killed the mood. I grunted as I accidentally put too much weight on my foot. Slowly, we inched our way down to the parking lot.

"This fucking sucks," I said.

"I am the one who defeated a vampire," said Killian.

"I wore him down for you," I replied.

Killian shook his head, "I would pay any price for a cool cup of ambrosia and a hot spring to soak in..."

"You and me both. I might trade the ambrosia for a couple shots, though."

We were halfway down the hill. The cross at the top of Boot Hill stood starkly against the bright night sky.

Killian leaned me up against the car and

opened the door for me. We both were looking at those graves in the cemetery, hoping none of them decided to spring forth with new undead life... again...

The moment we were in the car, I pounded the locks closed and Killian revved the engine.

"Gentle, Killian," I said. "Breaking down over here would be a very, very bad idea."

We slowly crunched our way across the parking lot, over the huge pointed rocks and out onto the highway. I waved goodbye to the entrance as we drove away.

I think I officially had my fill of the wild, wild west.

Chapter 16

"Okay, Mr. Smith," I said as Killian and I walked into MacKay & MacKay Tracking Other Side HQ.

I had been psyching myself up for the drive out to Ghost Town, but my voicemail was blinking at me from the moment we crossed over from Earth. There was a message from Mr. Smith to meet him at the office first thing. I guess there was no way of him knowing that we had already found the comb.

I made a quick trip to the local witch doctor, who fixed me up good as new, and Killian and I headed over to the office. I was bone weary from the all-nighter and didn't mind one bit not having to drive the comb out to Ghost Town. I tried calling my dad to get him up to speed on the 4-1-1, but he didn't pick up, as per usual.

The office was open. Seemed a little rude to

114

come in while the door was locked, not to mention illegal, but the more I learned about Mr. Smith, the more I got the idea he didn't wait around much for anything.

"Listen, we got it, Mr. Smith. Now, I'd like to give this to you to crush beneath something heavy, but I got this note from Vaclav..."

Mr. Smith was lying on the ground next to my desk, beat to hell, his little mouth opening and closing like a guppy gasping for air.

"Killian, call the police!" I said as I crouched down next to the old dude and started checking his vitals. "Come on, Mr. Smith. You're not allowed to die before I kill you."

"Maggie? Is that you?" he asked, his eyes barely able to focus.

"It ain't the stake fairy. Come on, stick with me."

"I was discovered. They found me."

"Well... these things happen," I said lamely.

"It is important you continue my work..."

"Come on, you're going to continue your own work," I said. My brain was racing. God, the blood was everywhere. It could have been vampires, but my threshold should have still been intact and, besides, it was broad daylight. I didn't see any puncture wounds in his neck. There were chunks missing from my furniture and deep scratch marks in the floor that made me think werewolves.

"This is much larger than me. This is much larger than my life. They stole the jade comb..." he coughed.

I got chills down my spine, "From my dad...?"

"No. From me. Here."

"Good. I mean, not good that they got you here, but good... that it wasn't..." I was blowing it in the "meaningful final moments" department. "Don't worry. We'll get it back. Where's my dad, Mr. Smith?"

"In Ghost Town. He's safe. Protected."

"If you are lying to me, I will hunt you down and end you myself, old man."

"Too late..." he smiled a pained, blood soaked grin.

"Who did this, Mr. Smith?"

"Vaclav..."

He paused, the end of the sentence trailing of.

I gave him a little shake, "Come on. Dying on me doesn't help."

He gasped, "You must... take your comb... to Ghost Town... your father is safe... hidden... you must... find the necklace... Ghost Town..."

And he slipped away. Just like that. One moment here, the next gone. Killian placed his hand on my shoulder.

We were on our own. We had a world of hurt

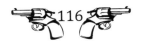

116

barreling towards us down the shotgun of life and the bad guys just showed they weren't shooting blanks.

Fucking double fuck.

Fuck.

Chapter 17

The cops had come and gone, zipping up ol' Isaac Smith in a body bag and wheeling him off to the morgue. I was completely useless as they interviewed me. I had nothing on Mr. Smith. No address, no contact information, nada. It sounded kind of lame to say, "I barely knew the guy."

Except I barely knew the guy. He showed up out of nowhere and paid in cash. I hated him, but I also kinda wished he wasn't dead. I gave the police the phone number I had and hoped maybe they could do some sort of a reverse trace and track down the guy's next of kin.

Killian was a sport and hung out with me through the whole ordeal. The claw marks in the floor and walls made it pretty clear I was more of a "target" than a "suspect", but it's just never fun times giving a statement, especially when you've got to "conveniently" leave out that you were

brawling with some vampires the night before and had smuggled in an illegal artifact that was sitting in your pocket.

The moment I mentioned that in his final moments Mr. Smith pointed the finger at Vaclav, I saw the nod of "case closed" pass between the investigators. Things wrapped up pretty quick after that. You piss off the wrong people on The Other Side and everyone sort of figures you get what's coming to you, you know?

After the law had left, Killian and I were stuck waiting for the cleanup fairy to arrive. It's best to be present. If you don't watch, they'll replace the cobwebs with rainbows and leave glitter all over your shit.

I spun slowly in my chair, staring up at the ceiling fans, "Do you think they got what they needed from Mr. Smith or do you think we get to look forward to taking our relationship with Vaclav to a whole new level?"

Killian rubbed his cheek thoughtfully, "It seems those combs are of great interest to a number of parties."

I stopped spinning, "Do you get the feeling we're missing something?"

He nodded.

I got up and walked over to a great big chalkboard my dad and I sometimes used to map

things out. I picked up the chalk and drew a couple stick figures. I was a tracker, not an art major. But the stick figures would do the job.

"We've got three missing combs."

"Indeed."

"We've got one missing necklace."

"Indeed."

I drew a little guy with glasses, "So Mr. Smith, over here, had some sort of grand master plan to gather up all these things and destroy them, hopefully to weaken the vampires."

I drew a bunch of vampires and gave them little fangs.

"Yes."

"And Vaclav just killed Mr. Smith, probably with the same werewolves who attacked Xiaoming and my dad," I said as I crossed out Mr. Smith and gave one of the vampires a little trophy.

"We assume."

"Wonder how that all came to pass..."

Vampires and werewolves? They do not like one another. It is like... worse than pirates against ninjas.

"There have been stranger bedfellows," Killian pointed out.

I looked at all the little vampires on the board, "The Empress had the combs and necklace made because she wanted to build an army.

Vaclav would want these artifacts, most likely, because he'd like to build himself a little army, too. But it's got to make him pissed, that one comb is destroyed, the necklace disappeared, and I've got the other comb."

"It would make me angry."

I bounced the chalk in my hand a couple times, trying to see what I was missing, "But why send the note? Why threaten Mr. Smith's life in exchange for the comb, and then kill Mr. Smith before I had a chance to hand it over?"

"As a message to you?"

"Anyone as old as Vaclav knows you can't kill your hostages if you expect to bargain."

"It does not make sense, but that is not unheard of when dealing with vampires."

"Okay, so taking a step back," I drew some more little vampires around Vaclav, "let's assume he is building an army. But why now? What's his motive? You know, besides being evil to the core and viewing the world as an untapped resource of food and entertainment?"

I snapped my fingers.

"That's it. What the vampire said in the mine!"

"You had enough time to chat with a vampire down in the mine prior to killing him?" asked Killian. "Was this before or after you served tea

and braided each other's locks?"

I gave him a look, "It happened WHILE I was killing him, thank you very much. I'm fully capable of multitasking."

"I am pleased to hear you have not accidentally grown a heart."

"Ha ha," I replied. "As he was trying to bite through my neckguard, the vampire asked me which side I was on. He asked me if I was in league with Vaclav."

"...which would mean...?"

"Which would mean there is someone out there who is AGAINST Vaclav."

"Are not we all?"

"I mean another vampire. This vampire that I staked must be part of a swarm of vampires hiding out in the desert that is against Vaclav. And they had the quartz comb."

Killian nodded his head and smiled, "I find the thought of two warring factions of vampires a pleasant one."

"Right? I love it when they decide to kill each other off! It makes my life SO much easier," I said, adding a whole army of little vampires on the other side of my board.

"Except that it means the strongest are the ones who survive..."

"Strongest yet weakened," I pointed out,

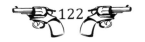

"because all their slightly less strong buddies have been wiped out. If Vaclav is desperate enough to start attacking folks in broad daylight..."

"It means he is desperate," said Killian, completing my thought.

I went in for a high five and Killian left me hanging.

"We're rockin' and rollin'," I said. "Up top!"

He looked at my hand and pointed, "I have no idea what that means."

"You don't know how to high five?"

"I am an elf."

I took his hand and slapped it against mine, "Moving on... Dad is hidden out in Ghost Town..."

"We should perhaps inform him that Mr. Smith will not be providing future employment opportunities."

I pulled out my phone, "I'll text him now and let him know we have the second comb. Hopefully someday he'll get it."

Killian gave me a thumbs up.

"Oh? You can't high-five but you know thumbs up?" I said.

"There was a Roman emperor who executed or spared his gladiators based solely upon the direction of his thumb," he explained, "and also there was a singing competition on television."

I shook my head as I grabbed the eraser, "All

that is left is to find the missing necklace and kick back, secure in the knowledge that we have screwed up Vaclav's day."

"I am particularly drawn to the notion of 'kicking back', Maggie."

"You'll kick back soon enough, Killian."

There was something else that was bugging me though. Sometimes my mom's gift of foresight rears its head to let me know I missed something important. Like that one time when it tried to tell me to steer clear of Mr. Smith.

I looked at the board, "I wonder who could have gotten inside of the secure apartment of a witch to steal the necklace, and then would be so bold as to frame a genie? Genies will mess you up if they catch you doing something like that."

"Someone who wanted the necklace very badly?"

"It's gotta be the other crew. It couldn't be Vaclav," I mused.

"Why so?"

"Because he's desperate. If he's desperate, that means he doesn't have the necklace."

Killian shrugged, "That would imply it was the other vampire group who stole it from the safe."

"Yah," I said, mulling it over. "I think that's it."

Something still wasn't right, but I couldn't figure out where the hole in the logic was.

"Any idea how we can go about gathering information on this other vampire group?" Killian asked.

There was only one place to go when you needed official information on a vampire turf war. I rubbed my forehead and sighed, "Yah, I do. It's not going to be pleasant, though."

Killian raised an eyebrow.

"It's not going to be pleasant at all..."

Chapter 18

"Killing your clients? That can't be good for business," smirked Frank.

I would've loved to wipe that shit eating grin off of his big fat ogre face, but I needed him.

Frank is the clerk at The Other Side's Bureau of Records. If there is a case, it's in his cabinets. The man has never heard of paperless filing. I always hoped that someday I would discover a way to butter him up and get him to play nice, but I usually had to fall back on just stealing his folders. Frank was the bane of my existence, but a necessary evil.

"Frank, I'm having a lousy day..."

"Sure you are, Maggie. I hear when the people you should be protecting aren't dying in your office, you're really busy running around the forest with a little fairy friend. Sounds like business at MacKay & MacKay Tracking is rocketing to the top."

I gritted my teeth and tried to just smile,

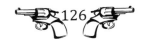

"Listen, Frank, we're both adults here. I'm a human. You're an ogre. Can we just act like grownups for just a second?"

"No," said Frank, disappearing behind his stack of paper.

"All I'm trying to find out is if there have been any reports of anything happening in Ghost Town. Then I'll get out of your hair."

I actually didn't give a flying flip about Ghost Town, but while I kept Frank talking about the place, the plan was that Killian was going to sneak into the back room on his silent elf feet and grab what we needed.

"Ghost Town? GHOST TOWN?" laughed Frank. "Oh, you're a scream. Yah. There's always something going on in Ghost Town. People getting scared to death. Kids looting the place. I have a whole file drawer full of cases, but you aren't going to get to see one sheet of paper until you finish up the other jobs I gave you."

"Well, I think that some info about Ghost Town might just help out with some of those cases, Frank."

He came back over and leaned against the counter that separated reception from his messy office, "Maggie, you might think you're going to trick me into giving you information on Ghost Town, but I got your number. I bet you have a case

you're independently investigating and just thinking you can use old Frank's time and energy to line your pockets."

"Frank, these files are a matter of public record."

"These files are in my office and that makes them mine!" he said.

I saw my partner's blonde mop sneak by behind the ogre. Killian's hand popped up just long enough to give me a little "okay" sign and then he disappeared out into the hallway.

I shook my head dramatically, "Frank, I can't believe you would accuse me of such terrible things. After all we've been through."

"The only thing we've been through is pain. Specifically the pain in my ass that I get whenever I see you."

I cocked my head, "That doesn't quite sound like the put down I think you're trying to say..."

"GET OUT!"

He pointed at the exit. I gave him an injured look that could have won an Emmy and slammed the door as I left for dramatic effect.

I sat down in the car with Killian, "Did you get it?"

He proudly held up a stack of manila folders, "Frank truly has a gift for filing. The ease of finding whatever information you are searching

for is almost magical."

"Right? It must be an ogre thing."

I started flipping through the pile of reports. There were a ton of them. I knew I was going to be up all night with this reading. You know, if it didn't put me to sleep halfway through the first page.

I smiled, "It's funny. He accused me of double dipping."

"Are you?"

"Killian, I am appalled you would think such a thing," I let it hang there for a minute, "Just because the police assigned me to find the same brimstone necklace that Mr. Smith and Xioaming asked me to find..."

"What a fortunate coincidence. So rarely do our own desires align so directly with the desires of those who hope to benefit us monetarily."

"Killian, that sentence just gave me a headache."

"How lucky you are that you get to save the world and get paid."

"I suppose 'lucky' is a word for it."

"The majority of the time, you do it for free."

"Don't go spreading it around. I don't want anyone to start low-balling my day rate."

"Your secret is safe with me," Killian smiled, "So, what does the file say?"

"It's... interesting..."

"What?"

I put the file down on my lap, "Well, you remember that little enclave of vampires we destroyed a few weeks ago?"

"Indeed. As much as I have tried not to."

"It seems that shortly thereafter there was a spike in vampire deaths," I clarified, "Not vampire related deaths. Actual vampire deaths."

I pulled out a handy little bar graph that some clerical peon had probably been forced to generate, most likely for some stiflingly dull slide presentation and handed it over to Killian.

"Could it be a slayer?" he asked.

"It would be awesome if it was," I replied, "but it doesn't look like there are any retaliatory human killings. Usually you see that sort of thing if it's a slayer going around offing vampires en masse. I haven't noticed the vampires unleashing a world of holy hell upon our mortal butts lately."

Killian leaned back in his seat and stared at the roof of the car. I could practically hear the wheels clunking inside his head, "Which would suggest some of the vampires were not pleased that Vaclav left them to die in the enclave... Perhaps we are truly looking at a vampire war."

"Exceeeept," I said, pulling out another sheet of paper and hating that I was about to throw a wrench in the nice little theory that was unfolding before us, "here's an accounting of some werewolf deaths."

"Really..." said Killian, looking over my shoulder. He grabbed the page and started scanning it.

"It says here," said Killian, "there were a great number of pups and den mothers killed in this attack."

"Which means someone pissed off the werewolves."

"It could be the vampires are fighting each other. It could be that the werewolves are fighting the vampires."

Killian looked at me, "You said that werewolves attacked Xiaoming's apartment while your father was there?"

"They probably thought he was headed over because Xiaoming actually had the comb."

"Instead of just information?"

"I learned the man is able to break all world walking rules I'm aware of and jump in the same plane. All the way from California to China. I would have assumed he had the jade comb, too."

Killian gave a low whistle, "Remarkable. I have never heard of any mortal with that capability."

"I KNOW! I'm hoping he does a one-day

workshop sometime," I turned back to the file, "So, either the werewolves attacked Xiaoming's to get the comb for themselves..."

"...or they attacked to get the comb for someone they believed could address their grievances with their enemy..."

"An enemy they already knew was stronger than they are," I finished.

"So, who would be strong enough to go after someone strong enough to kill a den of werewolves?"

"Vampires," said Killian and I at the same time.

"Jinx," Killian said. "You owe me a beverage."

"I never should have taught you that game."

"Jinx," Killian said. "You owe me."

I started up the car and aimed us at the McDryads drive-thru. Say what you will about McDryads, they made a great ambrosia smoothie. It was already mid-afternoon and dealing with the corpse and the police report and trying to squeeze some information out of that bastard Frank was making my stomach growl. I leaned out the window and ordered, "Two ambrosia smoothies, a Later Gator burger aaaand..." I looked over at Killian.

"A Shroomwich with curly fries."

"A Shroomwich with curly fries. That'll be it."

Killian started to get some coins out of his purse but I waved him away, "This one is on me."

The little pixie flew out of the call box to the window with my order written on the back of a leaf. Another messenger flew back to take her place.

I pulled forward and grabbed our food, which was inside a great big bean pod that had been emptied out and turned into a takeout bag. I handed it over to Killian who divvied up the goods and unwrapped my burger so that I could eat it with one hand while I steered with the other.

"I sure wish we knew a werewolf," I said.

"You do not?"

I bit in and tried, unsuccessfully, not to dribble ketchup on my shirt.

"God, no, they're disgusting," I replied through a mouthful of beef as half my sandwich fell apart on my lap.

Killian stared at me and remarked, "I am surprised."

I gave him a look and wiped my mouth, "I got friends in low places, but nobody that low..."

My voice trailed off as the thought hit me.

"But I do happen to know someone who manages a nice little bed and breakfast for the scum of The Other Side."

Chapter 19

We drove over the drawbridge and into the prison courtyard, the silent stone walls hiding the sentries who probably had us in their sights since the thought hit my brain.

I pulled up into the "intake" area, which is the same place where I dropped off the genie in the bottle. I sure hoped that Lacy was on duty. I didn't have the time or patience to sweet talk my way past some noob.

I pulled into a parking spot and we got out, making sure to lock the doors behind us. I didn't need any hitchhikers looking for an easy way out of dodge.

Lacy was at the counter filling out a crossword puzzle. She looked up barely long enough to buzz us in.

Lacy is blue. She is not blue as in "sad" but as in "actually blue". She keeps her uniform tight, her chi-chis pushed up to her chin, and her curly sapphire hair piled on her head. Dolly Parton, eat

your heart out.

"Hey Lacy!" I said.

Her attitude totally changed as soon as she saw who I had in tow. She practically purred as she saw Killian behind me.

"Is it chilly in here?" she asked as she leaned strategically on the counter, "because I think I could use some wood on this fire."

"Lacy..." I warned.

"What can I do you for, Mister?" she asked Killian.

"I had wondered why Maggie had never allowed me to accompany her inside," said Killian, taking Lacy's hands in his. "I can see she was frightened I might choose never to leave."

They stared deep into one another's eyeballs without breaking contact. I would have lost this staring contest due to the fact I couldn't have kept my eyes from rolling.

He slowly traced Lacy's arm with his finger as he spoke. She was eating it up with a spoon, "Maggie and I were just discussing certain aspects of werewolf mating rituals."

"I hear only the alphas are allowed to mate," said Lacy.

A devilish smile crept its way across Killian's face, "What do you think of alphas?"

"I think every now and then a girl likes to be

135

grabbed by the scruff of the neck and tossed around a little."

I cleared my throat, "This is really uncomfortable..."

"Maggie and I wanted to do some research, talk to someone with real knowledge about such things, but realized we do not know any werewolves. Would you happen to know any werewolves? Perhaps one we could talk to?"

"Just let me get my keys," said Lacy. She walked over to her desk drawer and grabbed out a great big iron ring. She gave me a look and said, "Maggie, you keep this partner around. I like him. Much better than you just showing up and begging me to let you into a high security area of the prison to talk to a werewolf. That was your plan, right?"

"That was the plan."

She shook her head, "You need to work on your approach. I haven't seen you since before you dropped off that genie bottle and disappeared."

"You weren't working that day!" I protested.

"Makes me start thinking you only stop by when you need something," She came around the end of the counter and gave Killian a good old look up and down, smiling like he was chocolate cake à la mode and it was her birthday, "Although you can stop by anytime YOU need something..."

She opened up the door to the prison, "After you."

Killian seemed only too pleased to oblige her, giving her a view of his best side.

Lacy hiked up her boys and followed.

As we walked deeper and deeper into the prison, I tried to make some small talk. You know, to remind Lacy that I was here, too.

"What ended up happening to that genie? Is he locked up in a can somewhere?"

"Abad?" she asked.

I shrugged, "Is that his name? I was a little more focused on trying to make sure he didn't squash me."

Lacy waved me off, "Abad ain't bad for a genie. You know, once you get to know him. We used one of our three wishes to make him tell the truth. Turns out he didn't steal the necklace, so we let him go."

I stopped dead in the hallway, "That would have been some nice information to have had passed along to me, seeing as how I'm the one who imprisoned him."

"Don't get your leathers in a bunch, Maggie," said Lacy. "You can handle a genie."

Killian nodded sagely, "I have the utmost faith in your skills of genie avoidance."

"Whose side are you on?"

Lacy shook her head, "Listen, we're not complete idiots. The witch found her necklace and dropped all charges."

"Really? So, that means I could have stopped looking for the necklace?"

"Well, maybe if you dropped by every now and then I could get you up to speed."

"I was busy. Trying to track down a brimstone necklace. That a genie supposedly had stolen. A genie who is now wandering around and really pissed that I stuck him in a bottle!"

"It's FINE, Maggie. We used our second wish to send Abad back to the Dark Dimension."

"And what did you use for your third wish?" I asked.

"Well, that's something for me to know and Killian to find out," Lacy said with a wink.

"I don't want to know," I clarified with my partner. "If you find out, don't tell me."

There was a buzzing noise and the next door opened in front of us. Lacy waved us through, "Okay, kids. This has been party and a half, but you're on your own from here on out. Don't go breaking anyone out of prison."

"You have our word," said Killian.

"I'd hate to have to use the 'I was glamoured by an elf' excuse in front of a judge," she replied.

"Oh, you have not been glamoured," said

Killian.

I felt the room heat up and Lacy started fanning herself.

"Now, you have been glamoured," he smiled.

She licked her lips and elbowed me in the side, "Give me a call if you ever need back up."

"I'll do that," I said, watching her as she left. I turned back to Killian, "Show off."

"It is pleasant that someone appreciates me for my charms."

Fucking elves.

We made it through a couple more locked doors and some bullet/magic proof glass walls. I unloaded my weapons and got myself such a thorough frisking I could probably cancel my next annual.

We finally made it into a long room with little booths for talking to the inmates through chicken wire glass.

The guards led in a long haired guy in a neon yellow jumpsuit. He was covered in tattoos and his skin was weather-worn. He was missing an eye and a couple teeth, his ear had a hole in it where it looked like someone had tried to tag him. Killian and I picked up our phones. He picked it up on the other side.

"Where'd you get that?" I asked, pointing at his ear.

"National park service. Yosemite. They tranqued me and tried to relocate me to Alaska. They never made it."

"Nice," I said.

"So who the fuck are you?" he growled.

This is why I don't like werewolves. A) they are assholes and B) they are assholes. There's this whole pack mentality and so everyone is always biting and scrapping their way to the top. And then sometimes you get outsiders like this guy looked to be. You don't get airlifted to Alaska if you've got a pack taking care of you. Lone wolves aren't anything to tangle with and I'd bet this guy's winning personality was one of the factors that got him kicked out.

"We're just two folks needing information on some stuff that's going on," I said.

"The only reason I'm talking to you is because I'm so fucking bored in my cell."

"Glad we could provide some distraction."

The werewolf stared at me with his beady yellow eyes. Sure, he was in human form right now, but you make that human/wolf transformation enough and certain characteristics tend to bleed through.

"What are you going to give me for talking to you?" he asked

"World peace...?" I offered.

140

He laughed, "Try again, sugar."

"No, she is not joking. Your information could cause world peace," said Killian so earnestly I wanted to give him a gold star for effort.

The werewolf leaned back in his chair, "This entire fucking dimension and the next one can burn to the ground for all I care."

Killian and I looked at one another. I hadn't really thought much about the barter aspect of this plan.

"What about if I said I was hoping to go kill some vampires...?" I said.

The werewolf began nodding slowly, "I like it when vampires die."

"Look at that," I said cheerfully, "we've already got so much in common. And if all goes well, a lot of vampires will die."

He bobbed his head up and down for a few minutes, as if carrying on an imaginary conversation in his brain, which he probably was. Finally, he seemed to come to some sort of agreement with all the voices, "All right, I'll talk, but you gotta promise to come back and tell me all about it. About staking them through the heart and watching the light go out of their eyes. About every moment they gasped and pleaded with you to just give them a chance."

"That's creepy," I said.

"That's what I want."

The guy was certifiable, but I needed the information. I shrugged my shoulders and said, "Sure. You've got yourself a deal."

Killian looked at me like I was crazy.

"What do you want to know?" asked the werewolf.

"Some werewolves are after a magical artifact..."

"I've been locked in a crate for a year, lady. I have no idea what the fuck is going on out there."

"Ooookay... um... we think some vampires and werewolves have teamed up and we just need to know why."

The werewolf leaned forward, suddenly really interested, "It happened then. They're going after Vaclav?"

"Who is going after Vaclav?"

"My fucking pack," he leaned back, correcting himself, "Not my pack, but some people I know who are in a pack."

"What were they planning on doing?"

"Just taking him down. Doing it however they had to. Those bloodsuckers have poached on our territory long enough. We can't fly, but we can bite, and our teeth can puncture through a vampire chest as well as any stake can. We just needed someone to get them on the ground for us.

We could take care of the rest."

"So no werewolf would ever team up with Vaclav, right?" I confirmed.

"Shit, lady. A werewolf would rather have sex with a cat than run with that fucker. The alphas would never allow it. In fact, they've already said they would never allow it. Any werewolf fool enough to join up with Vaclav would be out on his own."

"...like you?"

"Fuck you, bitch."

"Just asking."

"I never worked with Vaclav," he said with a look that would have knocked me over dead if I cared, which I didn't, "I just don't like people telling me what to do."

I raised up my hands in supplication, "You don't have to explain it to me. Like I said, we have a lot in common. Thanks for the chat."

He jerked his chin at me, which I think was his way of saying "no problem".

"I'll be back soon with lots of stories," I said, "of killing vampires and... killing vampires."

"See you soon, sugar."

He got up and gave me a little air kiss.

I hung up the phone and Killian and I walked over to the door to be let out.

"So at least we now know that our enemy is

the enemy of our enemy…" I mused.

"Are you really coming back to tell him about your vampire killing exploits?" Killian asked.

"Are you kidding me?" I replied as the door buzzed and I opened it. "That fucker is nuts."

Chapter 20

"Thanks for doing a ride-along today," I said.

"Finding a dead man on the floor of your office and speaking face-to-face with a werewolf will provide interesting dinner conversation at tonight's royal banquet," replied Killian.

"Glad to be of service," I said as I pulled out of the prison. "Listen, Mindy's hosting dinner tonight. Hopefully Dad got my text... or one of my many messages... and is already home. Mind if we swing by to pick them up before I drop you off at the Elfin Woods?"

"Do I have a choice?" asked Killian.

"Nope."

Killian smiled, "Your mother is quite delightful. I do not understand the friction between you two."

"I can't get away with ANYTHING around that woman."

Killian stroked my knee softly, "Perhaps we

should test her seeing abilities."

"Get your hand off my leg, elf."

He laughed.

We pulled up in front of my parents' house and got out. My mom ran her psychic eye shop out of the front room. The neon palmist sign was turned off for the night. Killian opened the fence gate for me and we wandered up the path through the teeny garden filled with foxglove and wolfsbane.

"What if your father is still in Ghost Town? Do you think he will be safe there overnight?" asked Killian.

"He better be. I'd drive out, but there's no way I'd find him in the dark," I shook my head. I hated when he took off like this without checking in, but he was a big boy, "He said he was all right. If he isn't, I'll track him down and kill him."

"Fair enough."

I opened up the door and hollered, "Hello!"

Mom called back from the back room, "Hello, dear! Lovely to see you again, Killian. When are you going to make an honest woman out of my daughter?"

Killian looked at me puzzled, "I find Maggie to be a very honest woman, Mrs. MacKay."

THIS is why I don't bring menfolk home to meet my family.

"I'll explain it to you later," I muttered to him, "Did Dad get home yet?"

Mom came out. She was wearing her good muumuu. The lime green one with the big hibiscus flowers on it. I guess that's what engraved invitations get you.

Her hands, unfortunately, were full with a tea service. I knew what was coming and debated just telling her I was going to go start the car. She came over and gave me a great big kiss on the cheek and put the tray down.

"Come on, we're going to be late to Mindy's," I said, hoping to talk my way out of one of her readings.

"We have to do this first, dear."

She poured cups for Killian and me and practically force fed us the Darjeeling.

"Listen, is this because I lost Dad?" I started, "Because he's okay."

She held up her hand, "Not another word! I told your father he needed to retire the moment you pulled him out of that dimensional rift and it serves him right for not listening to me."

"He called, though. He's out in Ghost Town and I texted him he should come home..."

"I know, dear."

"Well, so we were hired for a job, but the guy..."

"When she says 'guy', she doesn't mean romantically, Killian," she assured, patting his leg. I wondered what would happen if I just created a portal in the middle of her living room and left. She turned back towards me, stirring her tea, "White haired. Older gentleman. Yes, I'm sensing a vibration..."

"Yes. Well. He died. Before he went, he said Dad was okay, but wanted me to find a necklace and bring it and this comb... it's a long story. Anyways, everything is fine. If Dad isn't on his way back already, I'll head out to Ghost Town first thing tomorrow to pick him up."

"Oh, what fun! I love Ghost Town. Let me get my things."

"Um... we're going to Mindy's..."

She drained her tea and turned her cup over in the saucer. She motioned to Killian and me to do the same, which we did. I've learned over the years it's best not to fight these things. We lifted up our cups and she stared at the mess.

"No, we're not. We should get in the car."

She walked over to the hall closet and pulled out her Jackie O sunglasses and a big floppy hat.

"But Mindy is waiting for us..."

She smiled patiently, "Now, I see two paths before us. We can either fight for twenty minutes until you see it my way or you can just get in the

car. Both paths lead to the same outcome, so I recommend we skip the yelling."

I put down my teacup, pulled the keys out of my pocket, and headed towards the door. I waved Killian to follow. This was so not my idea of how this evening was supposed to unfold.

"If time is of the essence, I can walk home from here," offered Killian.

Mom patted his cheek, "Oh dear me no, you need to come with us."

Killian pointed in the direction of the elfin wood, "But there is a banquet..."

I shook my head, "You can't fight it. She's always right. Even when she's not right, she is always right."

"Oh, and dear, you'll want to get that," she said over her shoulder to me.

And that was when my phone rang. My mom waggled her finger at me to pick it up and be quick about it.

It was my sister's number.

"Mindy?"

"Um... Maggie?"

Her voice sounded... I don't know. Thin. She sounded scared and a little unsure.

"You okay?" I asked.

"Um... could you come pick me up?"

"Sure," I said, looking over at Killian. "We're

on our way over right now. Where are you at?"

"I am in front of a sign that says 'Ghost Town'. And it is really hot, but it looks like a storm is coming. The road doesn't look like it's been used in years. There is no one anywhere."

"Wait. Mindy? I don't know... Where is there a ghost town near Pasadena?"

"Unless Earth has grown another sun, I'm pretty sure that I'm on the Other Side."

"Fuck."

I turned to Mom and put my hand over the receiver, "DID YOU KNOW THIS WAS GOING TO HAPPEN?"

She sighed, "I told you to just get in the car, but do you listen to me? No. You never listen to me. And instead, you had to make it seem like I was being unreasonable. Am I ever unreasonable? Am I ever without my reasons? No."

My head was about to explode, so I just turned back to the phone, "I'm on my way, Mindy. We're getting in the car right now and are on our way to you. Find someplace to hide. We're on our way..."

I was babbling at this point and Mom took the phone out of my hand, "Mindy, just tell the ghosts you're a MacKay, and you'll be fine. We'll see you in a few."

And then she flipped the phone closed and

150

held it out for me.

Mom slipped her arm around my shoulders and gave me a bracing half hug, "It will be okay, Maggie. Everything works out alright in the end."

I looked at her and she smiled reassuringly.

And that was the reason I really liked having a psychic for a mom.

Chapter 21

With my foot on the pedal like a brick made of lead, we drove south from Mom's house towards the desert. I'd say like a bat out of hell, except there were hellbats all over the Other Side and they don't drive fast at all. It's hard to hit the gas with a stumpy cloven foot and short legs. Killian was in the backseat and Mom was riding shotgun. I hoped we got to Ghost Town before night fell, but I knew there wasn't a chance we could make it back before the moon rose and the nasties came out to play.

As far as the eye can see was a sea of red sand and boulders. There were tumbleweeds that will eat you and cactus plants that will pull themselves out of the ground to give you a hug.

Needless to say, I hate the Other Side desert.

I cranked up the A/C, "So, how do we move around Ghost Town without pissing anyone off?"

"You ask nicely," replied my mom, wrapping herself up in her muumuu. "Brrr... it is so cold. Aren't you cold, Killian?"

152

I shot him back a look, daring him to say anything.

Mom rolled down the window to let in some of the dry heat. I reach over and pressed the "up" button, "No! You do not get to roll down the windows in the desert! Window privileges revoked!"

I slammed the window lock for emphasis.

"Really, Maggie, we're in the middle of nowhere. What could possibly happen?"

A goblin threw himself against the glass.

"THAT!" I said, pointing. "THAT is what happens."

My mom started making little cooing noises and scratching at the goblin's little face as he tried to chew his way through the window.

"Do not encourage him, Mom!"

"Why, he's just the cutest little thing. Do you think he'd clean my house like Mindy's?"

"He's a goblin, Mom. Not a brownie."

She recoiled and made a stinky face, "Oh. They look so much alike."

"They look nothing alike."

"They are sort of the same size."

I rolled my eyes, "Yes. You're right. They're the same size. They're practically twins."

My mom waved her hands at the beastie, "Shoo! Shoo!"

He started doing all sorts of awful things with his tongue against the glass.

"Honey, he doesn't seem to want to leave," Mom pointed out.

I reached into the top of my boot and pulled out my gun. I aimed it at the goblin, begging him to just give me a good excuse.

He looked at the gun and looked at me and then let go of the window like a jumper whose chute just opened.

"Must you always resort to violence?" asked my mom.

"She is very good at it," piped in Killian.

Mom didn't even acknowledge him as she continued to snipe at me, "Really, dear, how is Killian ever to think of you as life-partner material if you go around threatening defenseless animals?"

I looked at Killian in the rearview mirror, "How many more defenseless animals do I have to threaten before you are completely repelled by the thought of spending an eternity with me?"

"Four."

"I'll put it on my to-do list."

"You crazy lovebirds," she laughed.

"Don't make me roll down your window, Mom."

Chapter 22

The outskirts of town spread before us as we crested the hill. Coming up along the side of the road was a weathered wooden sign that read "Welcome to Ghost Town = Population 0".

I pulled over and popped the glove compartment.

"Stake or gun, Mom?"

She sighed, "Neither. Really, dear. Walking into a perfectly lovely little town with weapons blazing..."

I couldn't have this fight right now. I turned to Killian, "Stake or gun?"

"I am armed," he replied.

He had pulled his collapsible staff out of regions unknown in the past. I had no idea where he was storing it now, but I wasn't about to ask.

"Well, here's a stake anyways."

I undid my seatbelt and flung the door open, aiming my firearm at whatever might want to jump out at us.

"Really, Maggie," sighed my Mom. She opened up her door and stepped out. "Mindy? Mindy, honey, are you here?"

Mindy came out from behind the sign and ran over to her, falling into her arms, "Oh god, Mom!"

She was shaking pretty hard and I let Mom take care of the mushy business while I scanned the area for anything that might want to make us lunch. Chupacabra, jackalope, you never knew what was going to come running out of the scrub.

"It is remarkable how much you two look alike," noticed Killian.

"Yah, except Mindy knows how to fix her hair."

"True."

"Don't agree with me," I threatened.

Mom was laughing and rocking Mindy gently, "There is no need to be this upset. It's just Ghost Town. You're a MacKay. You should have gone in and said hello."

I held out my hand and squeezed Mindy's, but kept my gun pointed to the desert.

"I didn't know what to do," Mindy sniffled as Mom wiped back her sweaty bangs and teary face.

I made a mental note, next time I hit town, I was getting a mini anti-monster kit to stick in Mindy's purse. Or a bazooka.

"How the hell did you get out here, Mindy?" I

asked.

She reached into her pocket. When she brought her hand out, it was wrapped around a pretty little jade hair comb, "This came in the mail. It gave me a shock and suddenly I was standing by Ghost Town."

Shit.

"Throw it down on the ground," I said.

She did. Killian watched my back as I walked to the trunk of my car and pulled out a tire iron. I gave Mindy a smile and then set to pummeling that thing into a lump of useless rocks.

"Can I have a go?" she asked.

That's my sis.

I handed it over and let her wail on it for awhile as I turned to my partner for a little powwow regarding recent events.

"Okay, Killian," I said, "somehow that comb was stolen off of Mr. Smith, transported back to earth, and then mailed to my sister. Any thoughts on why said person would do such a thing?"

"Either to prove that they can, or..." he got really quiet before confirming the thought that was bouncing around my head, too, "because they needed you here."

I looked over at my sister and my mom. They were just about the only things on several planets that would make me drive out to Ghost Town as

night was falling.

"What's your take on this being a trap?" I asked.

"100%?"

"That's about the same number I had in mind."

Killian stared down the road, "The options that seem to have presented themselves are that we can either choose to walk into their trap or choose to walk away from their trap."

Except that walking away wasn't really a choice, and I'm sure Killian was just throwing it out there to be polite. It was pretty clear someone was out to get me to Ghost Town. They were willing to kidnap my sis to make sure I came. We could leave, but god only knows what they'd try next. Someone once said that a wise man knows when to run in order to fight another day. Unfortunately, I tended to be an idiot when it came to my family.

"How about Option C? We go into town and just fuck them up?"

Killian shrugged as if weighing the choices, "Option C has a certain charm."

I touched his arm and lowered my voice. I didn't want Mom and Mindy hearing this part of the conversation, "Listen, Mr. Smith said that Dad was safe here. But seeing how Mr. Smith is now

dead and Dad hasn't returned any of my messages, I'm getting a little nervous that Ghost Town might not be as safe as everyone thought it might be."

Killian didn't even hesitate, "Then we must go in and bring your father to safety."

Killian and I stood side by side looking at the dirt road leading into the clapboard sided town. Its weathered false fronts were silhouetted against the sky as the suns started their dip behind the mountains.

"Maybe they have funnel cake," I offered.

"I believe I will accept your offer for additional armament," he replied. "Do you still have that wonderful crossbow you used to carry?"

"Does a troll have two stomachs?" I handed him my car keys. As he went over to check out the prize chest of weaponry in my trunk, I turned to Mindy, who was still wailing on the comb, "You can stop now. It's dead."

She stood there shaking and breathing hard, "You sure? Because I could hit it a few more times."

"Hit it three more times, then it's time to go."

She wacked the hell out of that thing and then gave it a good kick for good measure.

Reading my mind, Killian tossed me one of my reusable shopping bags and I picked up the beaten comb like it was a piece of doggie poo. It's bad manners not to scoop your magical crap.

I put it in the back of the car and jerked my head, "Climb on in. We've gotta head into Ghost Town to see who was so anxious to bring us all the way out here."

Mindy backed away. I could practically hear her little accountant brain chewing through the math of this being a smart move and figuring out we were all in the red.

"Are you sure? Maybe you could just take me home," she suggested.

"I don't like it any better than you do, Mindy, but the gauntlet has been thrown. We gotta go in. Otherwise, they'll come after us again."

"WHAT? Come after us...AGAIN?"

Mom took Mindy's hand, "What your sister is trying to say, although not very tactfully, is that it is important we go into Ghost Town. I have seen our future and I can promise no one in our party will meet an untimely end."

"I know you can't read your own future, Mom," Mindy pointed out.

Mom booped Mindy's nose with her finger, "You're right. But I can see YOUR future and it is a bright and happy one. So, just help your sister save the world this one time and I promise you won't have to do it again for awhile."

Mindy groaned, but got into the car. Mom

piled into the backseat beside her.

I was left standing there.

"Wait! Mom. How many times do I have to save the world?"

"Enough!" she shouted back, "Enough times. Now get in the car."

She reached over and squeezed Mindy's hand bracingly.

"Great..." I said.

"Just think of all of the lovely new weapons you shall have to buy," pointed out Killian, trying to cheer me up. He handed me a couple cartridges filled with silver bullets.

Which reminded me... I walked over to the passenger side and opened my glove compartment. I pulled out a sweet little baby blade. I think it might have even been packaged as part of a "My First Monster Under the Bed Kit" line of weapons, as suggested by the rainbows and teddy bears on the handle. If anything got to close, it would poke 'em through the ribs well enough, though.

"Think you can handle this?" I asked as I held it to Mindy.

She took it and nodded grimly, "Sure."

I could tell the last thing she wanted was to be stuck holding any end of a pointy thing, but we live in an imperfect world.

"Don't worry, Mindy. Killian and I will kill anything that comes close."

"I'm here to help, too!" Mom piped in.

"Mom will ask them very nicely not to be mean to us."

"You'd be astonished how just asking sometimes can smooth out any problem..." she reminded us. Again. The same speech we had been receiving since we were six.

"Mindy, this is just so you can provide backup if we need it," I explained.

"I am going to encourage you not to need backup," she said.

"Fair enough."

I loaded myself up with more weapons from my trunk to complete my ensemble of bad assery. Killian looked like he was outfitted for Armageddon, which was a good look for him.

"There is something about a Glock that brings out your eyes," he commented.

"Gun metal black has always been my color."

I opened up the driver's door and got in, "Okay, the plan is to go in, pick up Dad..."

"Dad is in Ghost Town?" squeaked Mindy, "Why didn't you say so?"

"... we pick up Dad and get out," I continued as I turned on the ignition and pulled onto the road. "We stick together. If anything moves, kill it.

You know, if it isn't already dead."

"This is almost like a 'Bring Your Family to Work Day'," said Mom, practically bouncing in her seat, "What an adventure!"

"As long as it doesn't turn into a 'Kill Your Family at Work Day'," I muttered.

We drove down Main Street, kicking up clouds of dust. The place seemed deserted, but that's because it was a ghost town. A pair of bats flew across our double-sunned sunset. I saw Dad's car parked in front of a broken down horse trough, so I pulled in behind, hoping maybe he'd notice we had arrived. I looked around for any signs of life. Instead, I saw a lot of signs of "not life".

The empty rockers on the post office porch rocked back and forth. I tried not to lose my shit as a cold wind blew by us, accompanied by the sound of horse hooves. Two shades sat playing checkers in front of the saloon. Except you couldn't see them. You could just see the pieces being moved and lifted, and the board being upended as one shade got pissed that the other one had jumped him all the way across the board. Rinky-tink piano music echoed down the street.

The ghosts of Ghost Town all died simultaneously from a poisoned well. No one noticed that they were dead for so long, it just didn't seem like it made much sense to go out and give them a proper burial. Their bodies were all lying around like beef jerky in the sun. And are still. But since they met an untimely end, all their spirits have been hanging around, too, just waiting for something to happen.

If you're a kid with nothing better to do, it's a hoot to come out here and get the crap scared out of you. But as a grown up, when you outgrow such things, they can literally give you a heart attack.

My keys jingled as my foot stepped onto the dusty main street. I was so over this wild west theme two days ago.

"Oh, it is just so lovely to be here," said Mom as she practically skipped out of the back seat of the car. "I haven't been here in ages. Just ages. I need to get out more often."

"I fucking hate this place," I muttered.

"Don't be rude, Maggie," my mom corrected.

Killian sidled alongside me, his crossbow loaded and casually at the ready as he whispered, "I do not feel comfortable here, either..."

Mom was over the moon, waving at empty sidewalks and broken windows, at all sorts of ghostie folks that I couldn't see.

"So glad I could help her get away from it all," I said, watching her have the time of her life.

"Do you feel your father or the necklace, Maggie?" asked Killian.

164

I closed my eyes and wiggled my fingers a bit. Sometimes the finger wiggling works. And sometimes it doesn't. Like this time.

"Nada. I'm picking up nothing," I said.

The first sun had completely disappeared and the sky was lit up with oranges and reds like an atomic bomb. The second sun was dipping dangerously close to the horizon.

We were about to lose the advantage of light, and that's when Ghost Town had the potential to turn from a quirky little tourist trap into a very unpleasant little spot. Not all the people who were killed by the well oh-so-many years ago were upstanding citizens. Some of them were downright criminal, and most of those folks were pissed about being trapped in this no-horse town for eternity. It took a lot of psychic strength to move stuff, but the poltergeists here had been lifting weights for almost a century. Not to mention all of the regular ol' Other Side things that go bump in the night. Out here, those monsters hadn't had the long arm of the law to encourage them to stay in the basement where they belonged.

The sooner I figured out what the hell was going on, the sooner we could skedaddle, so I decided to pick a building. Any building. I spun around and the first one in front of me was the saloon.

"Okay, kids, let's start there and work our way through."

I looked over my shoulder and only Mindy and Killian were standing behind me. Mom was wandering down the road.

I swear to god...

"MOM!" I yelled. "GET BACK HERE!"

She waved at me merrily, "I'll catch up! Go ahead without me!"

"If you get eaten by something, I am going to be highly irate," I warned.

She acted like she hadn't heard me.

I rolled my eyes, "You'd think I had brought her to a fucking amusement park..."

"It could be worse," Killian said.

"Yah. She could be standing here beside us."

"I heard that!" she shouted from down the end of the street.

Chapter 23

The saloon was swinging with a party of the dead. Dusty mugs were being lifted to invisible lips. Chairs were being thrown. A cloth wiped down the bar.

And not a single sound of a human voice.

It'll unnerve you. It unnerved me. Color me crazy on the whole "ghosts give me the heebie-jeebies", but I liked to be able to see what was coming at me and I don't think that was too much to ask. As a kid, our house was always getting haunted by some cranky spirit or another who was desperate to have a little chat with my mom. Waking up at 2AM with lights flashing on and off and doors slamming by invisible hands is enough to give any kid nightmares.

And now I got to relive old times. What a lucky girl.

"Excuse me!" I said as we came through the swinging double doors, clearing my throat so my

voice didn't crack. "We're looking for a live person that may have come into town yesterday."

Everything stopped.

Cards were frozen in midair. Cups were frozen mid-lip. I could feel all those invisible eyeballs on us and it creeped me the fuck out. Slowly, movement returned to the room.

"My mom will help anyone cross over who can give us a hand," I said, trying to sweeten the deal.

"Can your mother do that?" asked Killian out of the side of his mouth.

"I have no idea,"

"Maggie?" said my sister, tugging on my sleeve.

I turned to look. There was nothing there. I mean, there was probably someone there, because I could hear the sound of boots and spurs clunking their way across the floorboards to me. There was just nothing I could see.

But whatever or whoever it was, it stopped right in front of us.

"Think you can give us a hand... partner?" I asked.

I was greeted by silence.

"Sorry, dude. My mom is the one that can hear you guys. If you could just point me in the right direction, I'll try to take it from there."

The ghost picked up a poker chip and held it in front of my nose. Mindy's eyes were as big as saucers.

"Maggie, is this what you do on a regular basis?" she asked.

As the chip started to glide up the rotted stairs to the second floor, I replied, "Yah, it's not too far off."

I hoped that I was reading the ghost's signals right and he wanted us to follow, and not "Whatever you do, specifically don't come up here." I motioned to Mindy and Killian that we were on the move.

The ghost led us through one of the broken doorways. It was hard to tell if back in the day it was a hotel room or the saloon's cathouse. Or both. There was a rusted bed with a rotted mattress, tattered curtains, and a dressing table with a broken mirror.

"Homey," I muttered.

The poker chip floated to a window and the ghost tapped it on the glass. I looked over at Killian who gave me a "why the hell not?" shrug. I walked over to where the ghost seemed to be standing and peered around the edge of the pane. Killian went over to the other window and looked out, his weapon drawn.

From the second story of the saloon we had a

great view of the entire town.

The street was quiet. The orange moon was coming up and hung over the buildings like a pumpkin. Not like the pumpkin spice latte yummy kind of moon that makes you want to go grab something cozy and hang out with a good book. The kind that makes you want to start packing heat because a witch on a broomstick might go flying across at any minute.

I didn't see too many ghosts lurking around the streets yet, thank god. Moonlight makes them visible and they give off a silvery glow. During a new moon, you can only catch them out of the corner of your eye and startle yourself really good. During a full moon like we were having tonight, the opacity on their corporeal form is turned all the way up to 50%.

But at this particular moment, it wasn't the ghosts I was worried about. Which is saying a lot.

I was more concerned about the other manner of undead creatures infesting the place like, say, the flock of vampires coming out of the sky. As soon as they landed, they disappeared behind the abandoned livery. My guess was that shit was about to go down pretty darn quick.

The ghost started tapping the poker chip on the glass insistently.

"I see 'em," I said. The poker chip stopped.

"Can you eyeball how many vampires there are from where you're at, Killian?"

"Not from here," he replied. "I have counted ten vampires that have flown in, though."

"Any chance they are just passing through and not coming for an out-of-town convention?" I wished. Killian shook his head. "This sucks."

"Agreed," he muttered as another vampire dropped down behind the roofline, conveniently out of sight.

"Okay, we need a threshold, preferably one with locks," I said. I started scanning the street. Most of the buildings had their windows broken, probably by some dumb kids who hadn't thought that maybe someone might need a place to hide someday.

"What about there?" asked Mindy, pointing to what looked like a house. It had a great big false front and a wrap-around porch beneath a second story balcony. It's most attractive feature, though, was that it looked like it had a few less entrances than the rest of the spots in town.

"Done," I replied. I turned towards the poker chip, "Thank you. I'm going to see if I can find my mom. If we don't die, I'll make sure she gives you a hand. And if we do die, we'll be seeing a lot more of each other."

The ghost seemed to flip the coin, you know,

without any hands for me to see if that was actually what he was doing. I don't know if that was a signal that he was cool with what I had just said or if he was making a statement on our odds.

We moved quickly down the stairs and there was Mom sitting at the bar, chatting it up with the imaginary bartender.

"Girls! There you are!" she said. "I was just talking about you."

"Mom? Where the hell have you been?"

"Really, Maggie. Have you been hanging around sailors while I wasn't looking? The language."

"We have to leave. You can come back after we're done. Oh, and I promised this guy," I hooked my thumb towards the poker chip, "that you'd help him cross over."

"It would be my pleasure," she replied, rolling up her sleeves.

"Just not now, Mom," I said, grabbing her wrist. "Later. First we have to not die."

I dragged her towards the exit and Killian and Mindy trotted after us.

"I'll be back!" promised Mom, calling over her shoulder, blissfully unaware of the fact that we were about to be in more than a little bit of trouble.

I peered over the swinging doors and

checked the street. It looked like the coast was clear. I pulled out my silver stake in one hand, my gun in the other, and nodded towards the house. Killian loaded up his crossbow and nodded back. We sprinted to the front door, which, because luck is a bitch of a gal, was locked.

I jiggled the handle, "SHIT!"

"Honey, just knock," my mom said.

She rapped gently upon the door and it opened. Her face lit up and she started babbling, "Thank you so much, Thomas. I'm afraid my daughter has gotten us into a bit of a pickle..."

"Don't pin this on me. I just wanted to go over to Mindy's for dinner," I pointed out.

"You're right, dear," she said patting my hand before turning back to Thomas, "Mind if we come in?"

The door opened wider, so I figured we were good to go. I stood to the side, ready to provide cover as Killian ushered Mindy in to safety.

I could hear snarling and yipping sounds in the distance. Dollars to donuts it wasn't a pack of wild shih tzus.

"Get in get in get in!" I said as I pushed them through and shut the door behind us.

Inside, the floor sagged beneath the original old furnishings. Thomas must've been one hell of a scarer to keep a century of looters from stealing his stuff. The years had shredded the wallpaper and everything was covered in massive cobwebs and dust, but otherwise, things looked pretty good. There was a parlor to our left and a dining room to our right. The entry we were in had a staircase going up and a door on the far end which probably led to the kitchen. There was a great big, heavy Victorian table by the stairs. It was like Killian was reading my mind. He grabbed an end, I grabbed the other, and we got the front door blocked.

"Werewolves?" I asked Killian.

"Werewolves," he replied.

"Jeez, if it's not one monster, it's another..."

"Remind me why we didn't just get in the car and drive away?" asked Mindy, socking me.

"Hey! That's my staking arm."

"Girls, please," shushed Mom, shaking her head.

"Maggie started it by hauling us into the Ghost Town," said Mindy.

"Oh yah? Well, Mindy started it by opening up an envelope containing a portal creating jade comb."

"I don't care who started it, I'm ending it. Don't make me feed you to the creatures of the night," warned Mom.

"Maggie? Mindy? Is that you?" came a voice from upstairs.

I looked over at Killian. He stepped in front of Mindy and aimed his crossbow at the landing. I took out my gun.

"Dad?" I asked tentatively.

A figure stepped out of the shadows and there he was. Dad came racing down the steps, looking totally surprised at our impromptu family reunion. He gave Mom a great big hug, "What are all of you doing here?"

I lowered my weapon, "It's Mindy's fault."

"Hey!" she protested.

"What do you mean?" asked Dad, releasing Mom and looking over at me.

I holstered my gun, "Remember how you got that jade comb, Dad? Well, someone mailed it to Mindy."

She gave him a little finger wave.

"Mindy opened up an envelope and was dragged through to not only The Other Side, but way out here to Ghost Town. Found herself on the outskirts of the city limits just a few hours ago."

"That's impossible!" said Dad, going over and holding Mindy tight as if he could go back and make up for that little whoopsie. "I gave that comb to Mr. Smith."

"About that... Mr. Smith is dead. Also, we probably need to get our office reconsecrated."

"Maggie MacKay!" came a familiar and

175

completely unwelcome voice, ringing its way through the walls. Seeing as the walls were missing great chunks where the wood had rotted away, we were able to hear just fine without even having to open up a window, which we wouldn't have had to open either because most of the glass was missing, too.

We all ran into the parlor to look out. I remembered right. I hadn't heard that unpleasant rasp since a cell phone conversation after I had freed my dad. But you don't forget the sound of evil.

"It's Vaclav," I said.

"Shit," said my dad.

I didn't get my potty mouth from nowhere.

Vaclav stood in the center of the street like the bad guy in a Western flick. If he had been short, he would have been described as slender or slight, but since he was seven feet tall, proportions were on his side. He was dressed all in black with his cape thrown over his shoulder like Clint Eastwood in a real life version of A Fist Full of the Undead. Vampires tend to lose their healthy summer tan after all those years hidden from the sun. To be frank, they look like death. His white, cue ball head had jagged ears that looked almost like bat wings. His peaked black brows sat above his blood red eyes. He ran a pointed tongue over his fangs and smiled at me through the glass.

"If you are not out on this street with that quartz comb by the count of ten, Maggie MacKay, I will be forced to send my associates in after you."

I grabbed my dad and pulled him away from the window.

"Remind me again why you didn't leave Mr. Smith's file in the drawer?" I said, checking my gun to make sure it was loaded.

"ONE."

"Maggie, don't sass your father," said my mom.

"I'm not sassing," I mumbled.

"You were sort of sassing," Killian not at all helpfully pointed out.

"You're supposed to be on my side, PARTNER."

"TWO."

Dad gave a huge sigh and rested his forehead in his hands, "I should have stayed stuck between dimensions..."

"What are we going to do, Dad?"

"THREE."

I suddenly felt the presence of something on the more expired end of the meat packing date.

"We have company," I said.

"What is it?" asked Mindy.

I put my hand over her mouth. It was a

vampire. I guess the house's threshold was so old it didn't count for shit and I was a dumbass for not remembering to check for a rear exit.

There was a door at the far end of the parlor.

"It leads to the kitchen," said my dad in a low voice, confirming the worst case scenario, "which has three doors: one to the parlor, one to the entry, and one to the dining room."

I took the safety off my gun.

We had put ourselves into a nice little position to get flanked. I could feel the vampire trying to sense us, trying to smell us. I know the difference between being hunted and being the hunter. And right now, we were baby bunnies up a fucking tree without a paddle.

We needed to get to high ground and we needed to get there now. The stairs, unfortunately, were right next to the second entrance to the kitchen.

I only felt one dude, though, so I held up my finger for "one". I jerked my head back towards the hallway and pointed up. Dad and Killian nodded.

"FOUR," Vaclav continued counting, probably figuring we'd be quaking in our boots so hard we wouldn't notice his minion coming at us fangs out.

He figured wrong.

I edged up along the corner of the doorframe,

my gun in one hand, my stake in another. Mom just continued merrily chatting away with her ghost friend, Thomas, like there wasn't some rabid undead monster stalking us. I hooked her with my arm and pulled her behind me.

"Now really, dear. It isn't polite to interrupt in the middle of such a pleasant conversation."

"There is a vampire in here, Mom."

"Oh, well, that changes everything now, doesn't it."

I could hear the vampire's hand on the door handle as he slowly tried to turn it.

"Come on," I whispered.

Dad took charge of Mom and Mindy as Killian checked the entry to make sure it was clear. I was just about to push everyone into the hallway when the vampire rushed out the kitchen and into the parlor.

I fired two shots. Neither of them connected. That vampire was like a fucking ninja. He very well could have been a ninja back in the day. They're usually swift enough to kick a vampire's ass pretty effectively, but a ninja's gotta sleep sometime and those vampires are tricky.

I really hoped that I wasn't up against a former ninja.

And then the vampire tripped and fell on the ground. I have never heard nor seen a clumsy

vampire, but I wasn't going to ask him if he had a boo-boo. I pulled out my stake and got him before he even had a chance to say, "Who dropped this banana peel?"

Killian ran over to the door and slammed it shut as I wiped my stake on my pant leg. Mom whispered, "Thank you, Thomas."

"Did he just trip that vampire for us?" I asked.

"Let's just say he gave him a gentle nudge in the right direction," she said.

"Thank you, Thomas!" I mouthed.

"FIVE," Vaclav continued.

Speaking of five, I counted five more unwanted dinner guests trying to sneak in. We had definitely not made enough to feed everyone.

I motioned to the fam to stay still. I snuck over to the parlor doorway. I could feel the vampires had split up, probably to hem us in, and that one had hidden himself in the entry. I peered into the hallway and was just a few millimeters shy of accidentally catching that vampire square in the eyes and finding myself in a thrall.

He hissed and flew at me. I fired. Once. Twice. On the third one I hit him with my silver bullet and he crashed to the ground.

So much for the element of surprise.

We took off up the stairs. I fired as the three other monsters burst out of the kitchen and

scrambled after us. Killian took out the stake I had loaned him and buried one deep into the heart of one of the guys. He went down.

We only had two more kitchen vampires left, but I could feel there was a third vamp somewhere. I pushed Mindy in front of me as one of the suckers grabbed me by the heel. I gave him a kick to the mouth and hoped that I did enough damage to at least send him to the dentist for some cosmetic work.

He grappled for my knee and I kicked him again. Killian fired off an arrow from the crossbow he had been hauling around and got the fourth one, which was levitating in the air looking for a good opportunity to dog pile on top of me. I flipped over onto my belly and got my knee in between the vampire and my chest, and kicked him off. He went tumbling down the stairs.

"Maaaagie?" called Mindy.

I looked over. Seemed the extra vampire had decided to do a sweep of the top floors and had gotten there before us.

I pulled my silver stake out of my boot top and winged it at him. Boom. Straight in his heart. My sister stood pressed up against the wall as he fell to the floor with a thunk. She looked at him lying there on the ground and then got closer to the stake.

"Is that the one I got you for Christmas?"

"I use it almost every day. Thanks!"

"I'll make sure to get you another one."

"I always appreciate backup weaponry."

"SIX!" continued Vaclav. "Surrender the comb!"

"A little help, Maggie," called Killian.

The one leftover vampire hissed at us from downstairs.

"Oh come on, Killian. We can wipe this guy out in our sleep."

"Less talking. More killing."

I pulled out my gun and fired off two rounds into the vampire's chest.

"Done and done."

He let out a deep breath, "Excellent work, partner."

I blew the smoke from the top of my gun, "Piece of cake. What'd you say we go see what's going on outside."

Except that in the mayhem, I hadn't felt the new vampire enter. I heard a sound and saw the fear register on Killian's face. I spun just as the vampire jumped towards me. And then he dropped, right out of the sky onto the floor in a motionless heap. I looked closer and there was Mindy's baby blade sticking straight out of his heart.

I turned around, slack-jawed.

"Well done, Mindy."

"I always knew you had it in you!" said Dad, putting his arm around her shoulders proudly. "You're a natural!"

"Thanks," she said dryly. "Can we get into a room with a lock on the door?"

Dad gave her a kiss on the forehead and looked like he was just about to burst, "As soon as we get home, I'm getting you your very first staking kit!"

"You never buy me stuff when I kill things," I complained.

"We think you are special, too, Maggie," said my mom.

Family.

Dad led Mindy and Mom up the stairs as Killian and I gathered up our weapons and took the rear guard.

"Vaclav seems very quiet..." mused Killian.

There was a crack of thunder in the sky.

"Maybe he's off finding an umbrella."

"I hope he drowns in a two inch puddle," said Mindy from the landing.

I looked up, "I'll work on that, sis."

The upstairs was filled with rotting floorboards, which actually was good because there was no way in hell they'd support an attacking army. There were several rooms off the hall. We picked the one with a door.

As soon as we were in, Mom and Mindy stepped to the side while Dad, Killian and I moved a frickin' ginormous armoire in front of the door. Hopefully, we'd only have to last till daybreak.

I walked over to the window and looked down, "I wonder why Vaclav hasn't sent in more scary guys to finish us off..."

The town was completely empty. It was like Vaclav had never even been there. Dad and Killian stepped beside me.

Lightning crashed.

"Maybe that is why," said Killian, pointing at the street.

"Is that...?"

We all got really quiet as a round, tubby man with a fringe of white hair walked down the road, flanked by a pack of werewolves. Which is kind of funny seeing how the last time I saw Mr. Smith, he was getting zipped into a body bag.

"I thought you said he was dead," pointed out my dad.

"He got blood all over our floor, I had to fill out a shitton of paperwork, and now he's out for a stroll through Ghost Town?!? Son of a bitch!"

But there he was, just standing there, looking dapper and dandy. Except that his eyes glowed

yellow, which seemed to indicate that in addition to forgetting that he wasn't supposed to be moving, perhaps he was not in the sanest frame of mind. Around his neck was a yellow necklace of brimstone, half of the beads pulsating with light.

"And there's the missing necklace. How the hell did he get that?" I asked.

"Maybe if you had stayed focused on tracking it down like I assigned you, we wouldn't be having this problem," mentioned my dad.

"Not helping."

"You were looking for THAT?" asked Mindy, standing on her tiptoes to look over our shoulders. "That ugly looking necklace?"

I nodded, not really able to argue the aesthetics of the piece, "Hard as it might be to believe, that fashion emergency lets you control thirty-three souls."

"That is seriously fucked!" said Mindy.

"You're right, sis. It is seriously fucked."

"Vaclav!" shouted Mr. Smith. "I am calling you out!"

The necklace glowed. And Vaclav jerked out of the shadows, like a puppet on a string. He seemed to be trying to fight some sort of invisible force and losing. He was followed by his vampire minions, shuffling behind with zombie-like grace.

Vaclav came to a halt in front of Mr. Smith.

The vampire's face was contorted with rage as he spat, "You are an abomination, Isaac. Running with those dogs at your feet."

"They make rather lovely pets, don't they?" said Mr. Smith, leaning over to scratch one of the werewolves behind the ears. The monster growled at Vaclav as Mr. Smith spoke, "I only had to wipe out one den and blame it on you, and they were more than willing to join forces with me."

I turned to Killian, "Is any of this making any sense to you?"

He shook his head slowly, just as mystified as I was, his eyes never leaving the drama going on below us.

Vaclav looked like he might have actually recoiled from Mr. Smith for just a moment, "How do you speak of your treachery and yet keep those beasts by your side?"

Mr. Smith caressed the beads of the Empress's necklace with more loving idolatry than a hipster with an autographed picture of Ira Glass, "This is such an elegantly understated bit of jewelry, don't you think, Vaclav?"

"What is it?" he asked, with more than just a little fear showing through on his evil old face.

"Here you have been so concerned about finding those worthless combs of the Empress," laughed Mr. Smith, "So blind that you didn't even

realize that it was I who stole them from you right beneath your nose. You were so enraged when you saw that crushed brass comb, so sure that the MacKays had foiled your plans. You ate up all the lies I fed you as you stared at that broken bauble. Did you know that I was the one to crush it beneath my heel?"

Mr. Smith was lucky he had Vaclav in thrall because that vampire was ready to fucking kill him, but Mr. Smith wasn't done poking the old bear with his verbal stick, "You believed everything I told you and played right into my hands, my old Master. You should have done a little more research rather than taking me at my word. The power of containing souls is not held in the quartz comb. It is held in THIS!"

Mr. Smith held the necklace as lightning flashed across the sky and thunder crashed. He began to laugh, "Your ego will always be your downfall!"

Vaclav looked at Mr. Smith as if he was seeing him for the first time.

"It seems the pupil has taught the teacher a lesson. Now, my dear Master..." said Mr. Smith, smiling in a way that would make paint peel off a wall, "Bow before me!"

Vaclav leaned his head back and laughed, which was about as pleasant as rat nails on chalkboard, "Never!"

It seemed to be exactly the answer that Mr. Smith was hoping for. He held up his hands and all the stones on the necklace started to glow, "By the power of the Empress, I claim your spirit! I claim the spirits of all your minions! And so I say once more, bow before me!"

And that's what they did. Every last one of those fuckers. Every stone on the necklace began pulsating and one by one, those vampires bent down on their knees, casting their eyes to the ground. The werewolves rolled onto their backs, showing off their soft little underbellies.

"Swear your loyalty to me!"

"Oh Master Smith," whispered the army as one. "We vow to serve and protect..."

Mr. Smith laughed, surveying all that he owned. He walked slowly down the street, as if relishing the experience of defanging all these monsters. Next to the saloon was a beat up old wagon, the weathered remains of what I'm sure was once a lovely little snake oil salesman's setup. Legend has it that the owner was the one who accidentally poisoned the well and killed everyone in Ghost Town. Legend also had it that the wagon was totally cursed, which was something that people tended to respect on The Other Side.

But not Mr. Smith. He mounted the rotting

stairs to the medicine show stage. As he stood there, his pallor took on an unearthly glow, like a bad psychedelic painting stuck under a black light.

Just then, lightning flashed across the sky again and a crash of thunder shook our flimsy little shanty like it was made out of cardboard. The rain started pouring down in torrential sheets. It was stupid raining. Mr. Smith held up his arms and the lightning hit his hands, setting him on white hot fire.

"Come my children! Come creatures of the night!"

The werewolves got up from the mud and slunk towards him like they were a bunch of lower caste dogs, barely worthy of his attention.

"Come those who have fought death and won!" he cried.

And that's when the horde of vampires came crawling on their hands and knees towards the medicine show, like dancers in a Britney Spears video, minus the sexy.

Surrounding this macabre, waterlogged, flash mob was the silvery flicker of ghosts. They looked almost like floating, moving ice sculptures. They were young and old, dressed in the garb of the prairie. They seemed kind of stoked about what was going down like spectators at a cage match. I guess "specters at a cage match" was a little more accurate. I think I might have caught one of them hawking peanuts.

Killian gave a whistle, "Vampires, werewolves, and ghosts..."

"Oh my," I said.

It was going to be a show, all right.

Mom turned to a corner in the room and said, "Thomas, I know that you don't like the living to interfere with Ghost Town business, but my daughter is very good at these sorts of things. Could you let the others know it would be best to let her and her boyfriend..."

"Killian is NOT my boyfriend," I corrected.

"Which falls fully upon her shoulders because I, for one, find her quite attractive," pointed out Killian.

"Can it, elf."

Mom gave my arm a patronizing pat to shut me up as she clarified for her ghostie pal, "Let her and her 'friend' decide upon the best way to dispose of these horrible werewolves and vampires creeping around your nice little town. Those creatures are like cockroaches and I would hate for Ghost Town to get an infestation."

Her pleasant little chat was interrupted by the sound of Mr. Smith striking his hands together. An echo boomed down Main Street, knocking the host of monsters on their butts. But instead of

scrambling back to their feet to see if anyone had caught them tripping, they stayed down on the ground.

Mr. Smith slapped his hands together again and there was another flash of lightning. The vampires slowly rose and turned towards the werewolves, barring their teeth. The hackles of the werewolves raised as their muscles tensed. And then the two enemies leapt at each other's throats.

I was really stoked thinking that they were going to kill each other off and do all the hard work for us. But then I realized that wasn't what was going on. The vampires were draining the werewolves of their life blood. And the werewolves in turn, had bitten onto the vampires and weren't letting go.

"Is he making vampires?" Killian whispered.

"No, I think he is making werewolves," said my dad.

That's when the two pieces clicked together in my head. Vampires can only be killed when you pierce their heart and the werewolves weren't biting anywhere near the ribcage. Werewolves can only be killed by silver bullets, and unless the vampires had gone out to get some bling up in their grill, there wasn't silver anywhere around those dogs.

They weren't trying to kill each other.

Mr. Smith was making hybrids.

A hybrid would only be able to be killed by a silver bullet to the heart.

It suddenly made sense why Mr. Smith wanted the Empress's quartz comb. It would make the bearer impervious to silver.

And that would make the hybrids invincible.

"Aw fuck," I said. "He's making vampwolves and werepires."

Chapter 24

I turned to Dad and Killian. I felt like I owed them apology. You know, since they were probably the ones that were going to have to deal with my "oops".

"Sooo... the quartz comb is in the glove compartment of my car..."

Dad looked at me like I was twelve years old again and had forgotten to turn off my curling iron two hours from home, "And why would you go leaving an artifact in an unprotected car, Maggie?"

"I thought if this was a trap, it would be better than having it in my pocket...?"

Dad shook his head in disappointment, "No new stake set for you, Maggie."

Mindy motioned to me from behind Dad's back that she'd give me hers. I shrugged at her. It wasn't the same.

Dad looked back at the street, "I count twenty-seven monsters out there..."

"That makes sense. Thirty-three spirits for

193

the necklace, but we killed six vampires... This is good," I said.

"Good?" asked Mindy.

"Better than thirty-three werepires."

"Touché."

Dad pointed to my Honda, "So we just have to create a distraction so that one of us can run to the car."

"If we all run for the car, could we just leave?" offered Mindy.

"What's your rush to get home, kiddo? This is quality family time," Dad said, giving her hand a distracted squeeze, "Something good on TV?"

"Yah, it's a show called 'I Don't Want To Die Tonight' and I hear it is great."

"On that theme..." I said, "I think I might have the makings of a plan..."

"Do tell!" said Mindy. "I like plans. Especially when they focus on 'getting us out of danger'."

"Thomas? You still here?" I called out.

"He's here, Maggie," said Mom. "Really, you'd think you would have gotten SOME of my seeing ability."

"I didn't," I sighed, trying not to let this moment degenerate into a Greatest Hits litany of all my genetic disappointments. I turned towards the general direction of the room and asked, "Thomas? Would you mind if we used some items

in your house to try and protect it?"

Mom cocked her head to the side, "He said fine. Just don't touch the crystal. If you touch the crystal, he will haunt you."

"Understood," I turned to Mindy, "Okay, Dad and Killian will unblock the door..."

"I don't know if that's such a good idea," interrupted Mindy.

I took her hands in mine and explained very slowly so she would understand, "I need you to go through the house and find anything silver we can use as a weapon. The pointier, the better. The more stuff I can stab with, the sooner we can get home."

"Fine..." she said, slouching off towards the door to stand by the armoire.

"Maggie..." warned my dad, I think sensing where I was going next.

"Dad, you know you have to be the one to go to the car," I said as I threw him my keys, "Grab the comb. It's in the glove compartment. And if you can manage to get us some bullets, too, that'd be great. Killian and I will provide you with cover but none of us are going to last very long if we can't restock our ammunition."

I turned to Killian, "Killian, you and I are the distraction. We go after Mr. Smith."

"I'll go with your father!"volunteered Mom.

I sighed, "Mom, I think it's best if you stayed here to help Mindy."

"She will be fine. Thomas will take care of her."

"He's a ghost," I pointed out.

"This isn't about Mindy, is it?" She gave me a wizened ol' look like she was about to blow my mind, "You don't think I'm capable of taking care of myself? You should have SEEN some of the men who stopped by my table in Santa Monica."

"Mom, those were just creeps..."

"I'll have you know I fought quite a few monsters of the undead variety," she said, brushing back my bangs. "Where do you think you get your gift from? Your father? Lord knows, he wouldn't know how to take down a vampire if it fell on a stake he was holding."

"I have to say I have seen him take down plenty of vampires..."

"Please. I taught him everything he knows," she said with a little half smile, bumping him with her hip.

Dad squeezed her waist, "It's true. Your mom was a black belt in jujitsu. The first time I saw her flip a ghoul, I knew it was love."

Mom giggled as Dad gave her a peck on the cheek. I just shook my head. I didn't need all these revelations coming out of the family closet when I

had bad guys to beat up. If she wanted to get herself killed and Dad was down with it, who was I to argue.

"We'll talk about this later. I can't handle this right now," I said, pulling a knife out of my boot and passed it to Mom. "You two get the comb and destroy it, and if anyone is still alive, meet back here."

"How do you destroy the comb?" asked Dad.

"Just smash it."

"Really?" he said, acting sort of surprised.

"Right?!? Someone wasn't thinking of long term durability when he was putting this spell together."

"Well, that's fortunate."

I looked around the room, "Okay, I think we're set."

"Before we proceed, I would encourage everyone to take a moment to enjoy a particularly pleasing sight," said Killian, pointing. "Is that Vaclav?"

We all poked our heads around the window sill. Sure enough, fangs deep in the throat of one of those monster puppy dogs was everyone's favorite master of evil.

"Oooo... he is gonna be PISSED," I grinned. I pulled out my phone to snap a picture, "Vaclav sucking on a werewolf. This is better than catching him flashing his man-boobs at Mardi Gras. I'm totally putting this up on Facebook!"

"Maggie! Wait!" said Dad.

I was so caught up in the delight of the moment, I forgot to turn off my flash. And just as I snapped the shot, the light went off, revealing our location. The entire horde of biting, bleeding monsters flipped around and stared at us.

"Smile for the birdie?" I suggested.

Mr. Smith's voice rang out across the street as he peered up at us, "At last! The entire MacKay family in one place. You must have received my gift of the jade comb and all came out to thank me, just as I planned."

"YOU'RE behind the jade comb?! That's fucking bullshit!"

"MAGGIE!" said my mom.

"Frickin' bullshit?" I offered.

She pursed her lips and narrowed her eyes at me.

I turned back to Mr. Smith, biting back the words I really wanted to say, "That is an unacceptable revelation that you have... revealed... to us."

Mom nodded in approval.

"Now, now. That's no way to show your gratitude to such a generous benefactor," Mr. Smith tutted. "You should have come out to pick

up your father earlier, Maggie MacKay. You could have prevented me from involving your mother and your sister. But now that you're all here, why don't you come down so that I can get to know all of you better?"

I hollered back through the empty windowpane, "We're just going to hang out here until you're done with things, if that's okay with you."

"Is the all powerful MacKay family reduced to hiding in abandoned buildings?" he asked. He then started laughing and did not sound at all like the wheezy old man who has been asking for tea just a couple days ago.

"You're supposed to be dead!" I reminded him.

Mr. Smith put his finger to his lips, "Oh dear, I'm afraid that I forgot. It threw you quite off the track, didn't it?"

I looked at Mr. Smith and he smiled, sporting a pair of fangs I hadn't noticed before.

"I thought you were fighting against the vampires!" I shouted.

"What a naïve child you are, Maggie-girl," he laughed.

"Hey, only my dad gets to call me that!"

"And what are you going to do about it?"

"Absolutely nothing," I stated.

199

"Because you know you have no more hope of standing against me than an ant beneath my shoe?"

"No, because I have much better reasons for killing you."

"Name one."

"Um... how about that you're a vampire!??"

Mr. Smith held out his arms to his army, as if about to bust with pride, "We truly are the superior species aren't we, pitiful human."

"Suck it, Mr. Smith."

"Oh, that is my intention."

"So how long has this been going on, because it seems like just this morning you were walking through daylight to get blood all over our office?" I asked.

"Didn't you know?" he laughed, delighted that I hadn't figured it out, "I'm your landlord, Maggie. Coming to see you was merely a matter of walking up a few flights of stairs. Ironic isn't it that not only did your father run around the two worlds finding objects I could never touch, foolishly believing he was weakening the vampires' hold on Earth, all the money I paid him to do it came directly back to me at the end of the month. Every check you have written to cover your rent has gone to help me make my own clan of vampires stronger."

I turned to my Dad, "When is our lease up?"

"I'm afraid you will not live that long," called Mr. Smith.

"Double-crossing bastard..." muttered my dad.

"It really is quite brilliant, isn't it? But don't feel too bad that you did not see it coming. There are many more who are proving just as easy to manipulate as you. And you helped, Maggie! You slaughtered quite a few vampires in Vaclav's castle," he said as he motioned to the master sucker, "So many of his faithful clan will continue following him, no matter what I make him do. And those who have not forgiven him will watch as he, under my gentle guidance, further implodes. They may hide in the desert now, but soon they will flock to my side. They will watch as he engages in the most despicable acts in vampire history, never knowing that I pull the righteous strings of his humiliation. Perhaps I will even marry him to a werewolf."

"Whatever!" I shouted back, "So you're a political mastermind with a good head for psychology. You and every member of Congress. Tell me something I haven't heard before."

"Wouldn't you like to know how I got this necklace?" asked Mr. Smith, fingering the stinking glowing thing around his neck.

Oh man, I was going to walk right into it, but what the hell. I said, "Sure. How did you get that necklace?"

Mr. Smith waved a hand and out walked that witch of a witch the police had hired me to help. The one who had reported that her necklace, the necklace of her ancestors, had been stolen by a genie. One Miss Veronica Dubois.

"I'm afraid your tracking skills will no longer be needed on this case, Maggie," said Mr. Smith.

"Has SHE always been a vampire, too?" I shouted back, completely fed up with this entire conversation.

"Oh, no," said Mr. Smith, brushing back her hair, "she is still quite young. Only since I learned she had the necklace. Amazing what a girl will do after a few drinks in a smoky bar. She was quite obliging to invite me back to her place. To neck."

"Ugh, that's just gross."

"The timing with the genie couldn't have been better if I had planned it."

"Mr. Smith," I said, "since it seems you lost me a job by stealing that necklace, why don't you let us go? I have lots to do if you expect to get rent this month!"

"I would love to do that for you, Maggie, but it appears both you and your father are having car problems."

He pointed his finger and four vampwolves leapt up. I could hear the sound of crunching metal. Seems they were living out the dream of actually catching a car and were treating our family's vehicles like chew toys.

"Okay, so maybe I don't have that much to do anymore," I corrected.

"Son of a bitch," my dad muttered. "I just finished paying that car off."

"Does our insurance cover monster attacks?"

"I can't remember if I upgraded our coverage."

"I'm sure you could file this claim as an Act of a God!" shouted Mr. Smith, "You have so many breakdowns, Maggie... I am grateful that you were able to fix your tire in Calico and bring me that brass comb. I never would have found that illegal portal on my own. Being able to cross my armies over to Earth at will is well worth the price of that trinket."

My dad turned to me, "You used the San Onofre portal?"

"I had to smuggle a car and an elf and myself AND a magical comb," I grumbled. "What did YOU use when you transported your illegal jade comb, Dad?"

"The San Onofre portal."

Mr. Smith was still yakking away down

below. Dad and I both stood there staring at his minions, noodling through what folks would think if all these suckers showed up on the beach. They'd probably blame it on a nuclear reactor leak. They should be so lucky.

"As soon as we get through this," Dad said, "we shut the portal down."

"Deal."

The sound of my name dragged my attention back to Mr. Smith, "You never finished the job for me, Maggie. You were supposed to track down a quartz comb if I remember correctly."

"Yah, I've got it right up here. With me!" I said. I looked over at Dad and shrugged my shoulders. If Mr. Smith didn't know it was mere feet from where he stood, I wasn't going to tell him.

"This is going to end one way, Maggie, and that's with you giving me that comb!"

"I have a different ending in mind. It involves my family going home and us never seeing your ugly mug ever again. It might also involve some pizza delivery."

Mr. Smith pointed at our building, his eyes glowing, "Burn them. Burn them all. And when there is nothing left but embers and smoke, retrieve the quartz comb from the ashes."

The werepires hissed and flashed their fangs.

One ripped out a porch column and broke it over his knee to make torches as Mr. Smith started stirring up the sky. The clouds flashed with electricity and the thunder rumbled.

"Stay on the ground stay on the ground stay on the ground," I muttered as I loaded up my gun, getting ready to start taking pot shots at whoever gave me the first opportunity. I could not let those vampires fly. If just one of them dropped fire on the roof of this dried out tinderbox, it would be game over.

"Oh, he did not want to do that," said my mom to no one in particular.

"Anyone besides us going to stop him?" I asked as I aimed.

Mom pointed down at the street. As if with one mind, all of the ghosts of the city turned and looked at us, their eyes focused on our window. I gulped. It was like something out of my worst night terrors. And then, in one blue breath, the entire population disappeared.

There was nothing but silence. Then, there was the earthshaking crack of thunder as the lightning struck Mr. Smith's hands and jumped to the wood the werepires held above their heads. It caught and the werepires advanced, ready to set our not-at-all-secret hideout ablaze.

And that's when the ghosts reappeared,

armed to the gills. They formed a protective circle around Thomas's house and you could almost hear them daring Mr. Smith's minions to cross the line.

One vampwolf apparently felt he could take 'em, and stalked towards the spirits with a rippling growl. He pulled back his muzzle and flashed his canines.

And that's when a strapping, young ghost stepped up and punched him in the nose.

The dog went down with a yip.

Now, see, ghosts aren't really that dangerous to humans or werewolves. Or at least that was the story my parents have tried to tell me since I was a wee little tyke. There is an exception to the rule for poltergeists, who can move things around and can carry wicked looking farm instruments and smack them threateningly in their invisible hands like a bunch of them were doing right now.

But regular ghosts? Supposedly they are just shadows to the living.

But they're not harmless to the dead. You know. Because they're both dead. And unfortunately for the bad guys below, vampires fall into that "dead" category.

And unfortunately for Mr. Smith, he had just turned his pack of living werewolves into a horde of undead puppies.

Meaning my family just got ourselves an

army that could do some serious damage.

I could kick undead ass on this side, and the ghosts could kick undead ass on the other. And together, we could buy Mr. Smith's gang a group rate ticket to the Happy Hunted Grounds.

"Looks to me like perhaps this is what they call a golden opportunity," I said, rubbing my hands together. "Everyone ready to go take care of some business?"

Killian gave me a high five.

Chapter 25

We crept onto the wrap around balcony outside our window. The sounds of battle bombarded us from all directions. The werepires and vampwolves were getting their asses handed to them by the ghosts.

I, for one, welcomed our spectral partners.

Thomas had shown Mom where there were a couple of tarnished candlesticks hidden beneath the floorboards and Mindy had found his silverware collection. We snapped the candlesticks in two to give them an edge that could probably do some damage, push come to shove. Hopefully, it wouldn't take a whole lot of pushing and shoving to get them through the sternum of the bad guys. Dad was already pretty well armed. He's like me when he gets ready to leave in the morning. Keys, dark glasses, extra gun... But I loaded him and mom up with some backup weaponry, just in case.

I pointed at the car and Dad nodded his head.

He took Mom by the hand and they made their way to the edge. Dad crawled over the railing of the balcony, bent down and gripped the eaves to lower himself to the ground. He dropped the last few feet. He held up his arms and motioned for mom to do the same. She gave him a look and whispered, "Is this a cheap ploy to look up my muumuu?"

He gave her a wink.

I rolled my eyes and waved for Killian to follow me to the other side of the balcony. The one that wasn't hidden from Mr. Smith's view.

I pulled myself over and dropped onto the ground. Killian just jumped, landing on his cat-like elf feet in a perfect ninja crouch.

"Show off."

"You made more noise than a giant marching through the dry leaves of an autumn maple forest," Killian said, looking out at the battle on the street.

"Maybe for my birthday you can buy me some of those fancy elf shoes and I wouldn't have that problem."

"Your shoes are not the problem."

"Can we go kill some monsters or what?"

"After you."

Mr. Smith was still up on his medicine show stage, conducting his army like the head of the philharmonic. He looked like he had already aged

like, a hundred years or something, but he wasn't getting weaker. The necklace around his neck was glowing yellow. Mmm... warm sulfur... I bet it smelled absolutely divine.

He was distracted enough by the ghost attack not to notice us sneaking out of Thomas's pad. For a moment, I entertained the daydream that we could just fire a bolt through his heart and be home in time for Good Morning Other Side.

That dream lasted about two seconds.

As I motioned to Killian to aim the crossbow at Mr. Smith, the vampire turned towards us, his eyes opened wide. They were pupiless, just these two glowing orbs of light. I was shocked they didn't shoot lasers. He opened his mouth and let out a furious howl.

"Killian..." I warned.

Out of nowhere charged a pair of fucking vampwolves. Up close, they were ten times larger than any pit bull. Really, they were horses. Except dogs. Great big undead dog horses. With teeth.

My heart pounding with the first hit of "oh, I will be eaten if I don't do something right now", I raised my gun with its silver bullets. I steadied my hand and squeezed the trigger.

Both puppies dropped.

Killian and I stood there just staring at the vampwolves.

"I thought that would be harder," I said.

He shrugged in bewilderment, so I shouted to Mr. Smith, "I thought this was going to be harder!"

I needed to learn to keep my mouth shut. Really and truly. Shut my mouth. Because life sometimes has a nasty habit of giving you exactly what you ask for. And I asked for it.

Those two dogs got up.

And it got harder.

Killian fired his crossbow, which caused the vampwolves to slow down long enough to yank the arrows out of each other's sides. Sure, it left gaping holes all the way to their innards, but when you're already dead, I guess you don't have to worry about gangrene.

"The crossbow is no good," I said, stating the obvious.

Like linebacker angels from the undead Super Bowl, I heard a crunch as two ghosts tackled the vampwolves, buying us precious moments.

"I shall fire upon them to distract them," Killian said as he reloaded. "You pierce their hearts with your bullets."

"Do you know where the heart on a werewolf is?"

Killian pointed to his rib cage sort of generally on the left side somewhere and wiggled his finger, "It is around here... I believe..."

He was no help.

I raised my gun, "Well, looks like I'm about to get a crash course in canine anatomy."

The ghosts were holding the vampwolves for me to get a clean shot. I fired, but didn't hit the heart. I fired again.

Mr. Smith shouted over the chaos, holding up his necklace, "Thirty-three souls, Maggie! With every monster you kill, you come one step closer to becoming mine! I will own you!"

My hand faltered, but I fired anyway. The shot went wild.

"Steady, Maggie," Killian ordered.

It was like being caught in a macabre game of "Would You Rather?". We could either get eaten by werepires and vampwolves or defend ourselves and become zombie slaves to Mr. Smith.

My skin tingled beneath my neckguard, the scars reminding me of what it felt like the last time I had gotten bitten.

I had sworn never again.

No matter what, never again.

So I fired.

My silver bullet pierced the vampwolf straight through the heart and a bead on Mr. Smith's necklace faded to darkness. I braced to see who would be forced to take his place. Mr. Smith was looking straight at me and began to lift

his hands as he gathered his energy.

But just then, a silver specter rushed towards Mr. Smith and the ghost took the hit. The spirit's eyes turned to shiny blue as the bead around Mr. Smith's neck lit back up.

I suddenly realized what had just happened.

We were in a Ghost Town.

We were in an entire city inhabited by souls.

And Mr. Smith had a necklace that collected them. Unfortunately for him, the new soul he gathered was lacking corporeal form, thus rendering it completely harmless to those of us classified as alive.

Oops.

Seeing that I wasn't bowing and groveling at his feet, Mr. Smith cried, "What is happening?"

I fired off another round and hit the other vampwolf. As the bead faded, once again, a ghost leapt forward, willingly giving himself up to the Empress's Necklace.

Mr. Smith seemed to have figured out what was going on, too. And he was pissed. He turned to his new ghostie pals and shouted, "Attack!"

The ghosts ran at their friends, but it was like watching a playground game of tag. Ghosts can disappear and reappear at will. So, the possessed ghosts would charge, and their buddies would just vanish and show up a couple feet away to sucker punch a monster before vanishing again.

"Thank you!" I shouted to the ghosts as Killian fired a crossbolt into a khaki wearing werepire in a popped collar polo shirt. As I followed it up with a silver bullet through the chest, I felt like I had really done the world a favor.

A ghost in a ten gallon hat and a shiny sheriff's badge on his chest slowly appeared from thin air in front of me. He pointed at an elderly looking ghost who hobbled towards Mr. Smith to take a place on the necklace. I'm not sure who was grinning more, me or the sheriff, at the thought of Mr. Smith having THAT guy in his army. The sheriff tipped his hat and gave me a wink before disappearing.

Maybe ghosts weren't so bad after all.

"I promise my mom will send all of you home once we're done!" I shouted.

A silent cheer seemed to move through the town as translucent arms were raised and fists were pumped to the sky. And then those fists went back to punching.

Speaking of my mom, I wondered how she was doing. I turned around and there she was, muumuu flying, as she drop kicked a werepire and staked the bloodsucker with Thomas's candlestick. Dad finished the monster off with his gun.

"How can this be happening?" screamed Mr.

214

Smith as he lost another bead to a worthless ghost warrior.

"I got a clue for you right here!" I shouted at Mr. Smith, "My mom! With a candlestick! In the middle of the fucking street!"

I gave her a thumbs up.

She paused to tuck her hairdo back into place and gave me a wink.

I fired another shot and got a vampwolf who was trying to tear his way through my protective wall of ghosts, then took down a werepire Killian had prepped for me by pinning him to the wall with a crossbow bolt.

And that's when I felt an arm across my throat as fangs struck my neckguard. I bent and flipped the werepire over my head. Hulk Hogan eat your heart out.

Scrabbling in the dirt was that lying witch of a woman, one Miss Veronica DuBois, who evidently had decided I was on tonight's menu. She leapt up with her claws out, a furious ball of white satin and spit. She rushed towards me and I barely managed to sidestep her. As she passed, she ripped at me with her nails and caught my arm.

She stopped to lick my blood off her finger.

"O positive?" she purred.

"Oh, I'm pretty negative, bitch."

I threw my silver stake at her and it caught her right shoulder. She staggered back as it impaled her, but then she smiled.

"Men have been looking for my heart for years, but not one was ever idiot enough to think it was there," she said, as she reached over to grasp the stake and pull it out.

"Really?" I replied. "Sounds like you've got some daddy issues. I know just the person to help resolve them."

And my dad shot her straight through the heart. The eerie glow faded from her eyes as the bead released her and she fell to the ground.

"Father knows best," I said.

Dad lifted his gun and blew the smoke off the muzzle like some sort of badass. Which he was.

"Thanks, Dad," I said as I ran to retrieve my favorite stake.

"Nobody gets away with trying to bite my girl."

We were interrupted by a sound that rang out down the street. My mom cried, "WILLIAM!"

Both Dad and I turned. Roaring with rage, Mr. Smith had decided to sic his entire army on Mom - ghosts, werepires, vampwolves, and all.

The whole world seemed to slow as I saw that wave of fangs and teeth roll towards her like a tidal wave.

Dad was off like a rocket. Mom was hurling everything she could find at her attackers. The remaining ghosts gathered as one host to form another worldly chain of protection. Killian was at my side in an instant, and shoulder-to-shoulder, we opened fire.

My dad got to Mom just as the monsters joined in battle with the ghosts. He grabbed her wrist and they ran to the car. He ripped open the door and pushed her inside. They both jumped in, locking the door behind them.

Sure, the wheels were missing and the bumper was nowhere to be seen. And yes, the engine was scattered all over the street. But the cage of the car looked like it would hold for a few minutes. My dad looked at me and I realized what he was doing. He and Mom were baiting the trap. With all the monsters focused on them, all I had to do was pick off the beasts as they descended upon the car.

Dad gave me a wink.

It should have been easier than shooting fish in a barrel. Unfortunately, if you are going to start shooting fish, it helps to have ammunition.

"I'm out of bullets, Killian," I said, my gun clicking.

"I ran out of arrows two vampires ago," he admitted.

Mr. Smith started laughing a low and sinister sound that grew with each breath.

"Did I hear correctly? Did I hear that the mighty Maggie MacKay is as defenseless as a fawn in the field? KILL HER!" he shouted, pointing his hand towards me and giving his army the command to charge.

I looked at Killian and Killian looked at me and we tore towards the closest building, which happened to be the saloon. We burst through the swinging doors when I heard my sister's voice.

"Over here!" shouted Mindy. "Come and get me!"

I peered out from the doorway. She had climbed out the window of Thomas's house and stood on the 2nd story balcony, taunting Mr. Smith with the child-sized, unicorn decorated knife I had given her in case we needed backup.

"How did you get up there?" asked Mr. Smith, with a bit of wonder and astonishment in his voice.

The pieces clicked in my brain. He knew I had a sister, but I don't think he knew I had a twin sister.

"Jade comb!" she lied.

The pack advancing upon us turned and began stalking their way towards her.

"Don't come closer!" she said, "or I will destroy it!"

218

"Always think you have the upper hand, don't you?" said Mr. Smith. He pulled out an old fashioned peacemaker with a pretty mother-of-pearl handle and, without blinking an eye, shot one of his werepires.

The bloodsucker went down. And freed up an empty stone on the necklace.

Mr. Smith pointed his hand at my sister and I saw Mindy's eyes turn golden. Her arms dropped limply to her sides. Her face went blank. It was like her soul had been sapped out of her. Because it had.

"MINDY!" cried my mom, opening up the car door and spilling out onto the street.

"MINDY?" shouted Mr. Smith, his face turning from smug satisfaction to a snarl, "You are Maggie's brat sister? You shall DIE!"

He lifted his gun to shoot my sister. My heart caught in my throat. Complete instinct kicked in and I threw myself out of the saloon, screaming, "NO!"

I raced straight at Mr. Smith. I was going to kill that fucker if it was the last thing I ever did.

Faced with offing my sister and getting offed by me, he turned his gun and killed another werepire.

And then he held out his hand, locking eyes with mine, and I felt the thrall descend

like a firestorm.

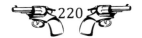

Chapter 26

Being put under a thrall is not the most unpleasant experience I've ever had. Your brain sort of empties out and your body feels like it's been shot full of Novocain. I couldn't really lift my arms or legs, but that felt okay. I didn't really care much about anything. Sure, there was a little voice screaming in my head that I needed to move, to run, to fight, but that pushy little voice was harshing my mellow. It seemed to make so much more sense to just ignore it.

The world was covered in a haze of gold, as if someone had put yellow sunglasses over my eyes. I heard words, or rather the garbled sound of words, but I couldn't make sense of it. The only voice I could hear clear as a bell was Mr. Isaac Smith.

I saw my parents run out from behind my wreck of a car, shouting something. All I heard was Mr. Smith shout, "Move one step closer and both your daughters die! That goes for you, too, elf!"

It looked like some big blonde guy with pointy ears was trying to sneak over to a house. Watching him was like watching someone run through water. That annoying voice in my head mentioned his name was Killian before I told the voice to shut up again.

But with the knowledge of the name, the world got a little clearer.

"What happened?" Killian seemed to ask my family. He sounded weird and echoey.

"He got them," said my mom, her voice bouncing around in my skull. "I don't know how, but Isaac got them."

"Step to the edge, Mindy MacKay!" commanded Mr. Smith.

The thrall was easing. I was starting to be able to think on my own again. I still couldn't move or speak, but I could think. I was horrified as I watched my sister walk towards the edge of the balcony. I knew she shouldn't. I knew that she should stay as close to the safety of the window as she could, but she started shuffling forward like a slow moving zombie in a bad 1970s film.

"You must help her!" my mom shouted at Killian.

"Which one?" he asked.

Mr. Smith turned to me, "Open up a portal, Maggie! Open a portal to The Dark Dimension!

Bring forth a genie to do my bidding!"

Listen, there are a mess of dimensions in the universe. The Other Side had enough teeth for my taste, but there were some dimensions that held even nastier things. Dimensions, like say, The Dark Dimension. Rule numero uno is that you leave that dimension alone. But my hands raised up against my will and I found myself gathering the energy to invite one of those creatures over for poker night.

"Your necklace is filled, Isaac!" shouted my dad. "You can't control this!"

"How helpful that you pointed that out! I shall have to create some room," said Mr. Smith, pointing his guns, one at me and one at my sister. "You'll only have time to save one of your daughters, William MacKay! Which will it be? Choose wisely!"

"Stop!" cried my dad.

"Open the portal, Maggie!" ordered Mr. Smith.

The wind began swirling around me and the lightning crackled.

"Maggie! Don't!" Killian yelled as he started to run.

Lightning struck my fingers as my mouth formed the words, "By the power within me, I open a portal to the Dark Dimension!"

I screamed, lifting my forearms to the sky like

I was some sort of frickin' messiah. I saw the air start to shimmer. Mr. Smith looked thrilled to pieces.

But I had learned a thing or two from working with Killian and those tricky elves. When you make a wish, it's really important to make sure you have all of the loop holes covered. And Mr. Smith's command was not tight. That little voice inside my head had a couple suggestions for a few extra words I could add.

"I call forth the Genie Abad! Come! Obey the power of the EMPRESS'S NECKLACE!" I called.

And that was when Mr. Smith fired both his guns.

But my family was already on it.

While Mr. Smith was distracted by my light show, Killian had vaulted through the air on his magical pole. He slammed into Mindy and knocked her down. The boards collapsed beneath them and, crashing, they fell through to the porch below and disappeared beneath a pile of rubble.

Dad couldn't outrun a bullet. Instead, he threw me a transparent piece of rock. A very important piece of transparent rock.

The quartz comb.

It hit my hand and I held on.

The moment it touched me, the comb made me impervious to all silver. Including silver bullets. Which is what Mr. Smith was firing.

His shot pinged harmlessly off my sternum, right over where my heart is supposed to be.

The unfortunate effect for Mr. Smith was that the necklace did not have the free bead that he needed to capture the genie I had just called.

And, as karma would have it, the guy who showed up was the very same genie I had bottled up.

I had told Genie Abad as we had stood in that alleyway that I would try to help him find the necklace, and he didn't believe me. And here I had gotten it back without him having to salt the Earth or burn creation to the ground. Was I a team player or what?

The genie's eyes were the first to appear. They were slits of rage. The next thing to appear was his row of knife shaped teeth, parted slightly as a growl emerged from his throat like a tiger getting ready to pounce. As his blue form emerged from the portal and solidified on the plane of The Other Side, he just happened to land right in front of Mr. Smith, the man who had tried to frame him, the man who was responsible for him getting bottled, the man who just happened to have the Empress's necklace hanging around his neck.

The wheels in Mr. Smith's head finally caught up with current events and he realized the genie

he had been so anxious to enslave knew what he was up to. You could almost see Mr. Smith gulp through all his bearded double chins.

And, what a shame, Mr. Smith had filled up all of the beads with souls and most of them were useless ghosts.

"I wish I had some fucking popcorn right now," I heard my dad say.

"You stole the necklace!" roared the genie.

"MacKay! Open the portal! Send this genie back to the side that he belongs! Seal it behind him so that he can never return!" cried Mr. Smith as, hands shaking, he tried to reload his gun. The genie was coming at him fast.

"Which MacKay?" shouted back my dad. "Cuz I ain't doing shit."

"Maggie! Maggie MacKay, shut the portal! Get rid of the genie!"

And because I was one of the greatest portal makers in all of the universes, you know, next to my dad, AND I was still under the thrall of the brimstone necklace, I had to do what Mr. Smith wanted. But, unfortunately for Mr. Smith, he didn't mention how fast he wanted it done, so I took my sweet ol' time.

The genie reached out with his clawed fingers and ripped the necklace from Mr. Smith's throat. Mr. Smith fell to the ground, in horror, just

226

as I got around to sucking the genie into my portal, never to be seen on the Other Side again. The genie glanced at me as he left. Dare I say I saw a glimmer of gratitude in those beady little eyes? Probably not. He was a genie, after all.

But now some real serious shit was about to go down.

The stupor left me and I started swaying in place before collapsing like a load of laundry. My legs were like jello. It was official. The world could end. I was spent. Mom ran over and wrapped me up in her arms.

I looked up as the binding dropped off the werepires and the vampwolves. And lordiedoo, they were not happy campers.

They stood there on the battleground, hissing and growling at each other, circling as if not quite sure who hated who more.

After a little discussion, though, it turned out that they all hated Mr. Smith the best.

They turned towards that sad, sorry little vampire man who had tried to control the world. A man who had, in fact, turned one of the most powerful vampires in several worlds into a werepire.

A werepire who was now not under his control.

A sneer rippled across Vaclav's lips.

227

Now, there was a brief moment when Vaclav noticed I was still breathing. I wouldn't say he was happy to see me, but I could tell he wasn't going to eat me. I would have liked to have pretended it was out of respect for the fact I had released him from his thrall, but more likely it was just because he wanted to tear into Mr. Smith more.

But I still wanted to kill him. I still wanted to kill him a lot. This was the vampire that tried to tear down the boundary between Earth and The Other Side. This was the vampire who partnered with my evil uncle. This was the vampire who sent his minions to kill me more times than I could count and went after my family.

But I was beat. I don't know how the werepires could still stand after coming out of that thrall. I don't think I could pull up my arm to stake the guy if he fell on me. And it pissed me off.

I think Mom must've read my mind, though, because she smoothed back my hair and whispered, "It's okay. You'll get him."

Vaclav paused for just a moment as he looked at me, and he then hissed a promise, "We shall meet again, Maggie MacKay."

I gave him a little finger wave, "I'll count the moments."

Vaclav spat something phlegmy at his minions and pointed his hand at Mr. Smith. The

chap fell to his knees and started begging as a flock of werepires swept around him. They took off into the sky, dangling him by his feet and tossing him around like a basketball, you know, a slightly terrified and totally uncooperative basketball. Several of the werepires decided this celebration deserved an escort, and they transformed into hairy bats and took turns biting chunks of flesh out of poor, pitiful Isaac Smith.

The vampwolves, not wanting to be left out of all the fun, tore out of town in hot pursuit, howling at the moon as they ran.

"Don't forget to send a forwarding address, Mr. Smith!" I said, "Rent is due in a week!"

Mom kissed my forehead, "Smartass."

It felt so good to just lie there, but Dad was over at the house, pulling large pieces of wood away from where Mindy and Killian fell. I decided I should probably check to see if they were still alive. Mom helped me to my feet and held my elbow as I hobbled over.

"They're just fine," insisted my mom. "I saw this in the tea leaves. They're a little sore, but nothing worse than what I've seen you and your dad come home with."

I didn't see how. Mindy and Killian had not just broken through the ceiling, but the rotted boards of the porch had given way, too, and they

had fallen through the floorboards onto the ground beneath. I was expecting at least one of them was going to need a cast.

"Grab an end," said my dad as we got there.

I guess getting your soul chewed up by an evil, undead mastermind bought a girl no sympathy.

As we lifted the last board off the top of the hole, there were Mindy and Killian, camped out on the rubble.

"Is it safe to come out yet?" she asked.

"Sure is, Mindy-lou," said my dad, holding out his arms to her.

She sat up and grasped both his hands as he lifted her and walked her over to Mom.

I leaned over the hole and looked down at Killian. He rested his head in the crook of his arm and smiled a sleepy smile at me.

"Resting on the job again, Killian?"

"I find sleeping through battle is a lovely way to spend it," he replied. "I see you are not dead. Well done. I suppose this means I can look forward to you trying to get me killed again in the future."

"What can I say? Some guys don't have any luck."

"Oh, I think perhaps one day I shall get lucky."

"In your dreams, elf," I said, holding out my hand to him.

He grasped it and let me pull him out of the hole.

"Thanks for saving my sister," I said.

He brushed back a wisp of my hair, "What else are sidekicks for?"

As we walked out into the center of Main Street, the ghosts of Ghost Town began to gather in a clump and drift towards our group, their figures flickering palely. I knew from my mom's stories that the first rays of the morning sun would make them invisible again, but for the moment, we could see them all.

The sheriff stood at the front of the mob. I brushed my hands on my pants getting ready to shake his hand and then remembered you can't do that with a ghost, so I just smiled and said, "Thank you. You will always have friends in the MacKay household."

And it was sincere. Maggie MacKay, ghost-a-phobic magical tracker was making peace with her childhood monsters. I suppose stranger things have happened. I couldn't think of any, but I suppose there had to be something.

The sheriff started talking and motioning to the people around him. I stopped him, "I can't hear you. Mom?"

She stepped forward as the sheriff continued and she translated for us, "He said that he was just doing his job. And he called you 'ma'am', Maggie. He's so polite, isn't he? He says that they didn't like all of these vampires and werewolves coming in and taking over their town and everyone is grateful that we were here to clear them out."

The crowd gave a silent cheer, throwing their hats in the air and do-si-doing in the street.

The sheriff held up his hands like he was trying to quiet them down. Personally, I would have preferred if they spoke up. He looked at his feet and kicked the dusty road like he had to gather up his courage. He pushed back his hat and motioned to the crowd.

Mom began beaming and then shushed him, "Of course! Of COURSE! Why, it would be my pleasure! It is the least I can do."

"What's going on, Mom?" Mindy asked.

"We're going to have to be here just a little while longer," she said, giving Mindy a kiss on the temple, "The sheriff said the reason that everyone was so willing to lend a hand is that they are all rather tired of being Ghost Town ghosts and they want to cross over. Do you girls think you can busy yourselves a bit while I help them out?"

I smiled and gave a little salute to the sheriff. He was one dead guy all right by me. I socked

Mindy in the arm, "Come on, sis. One of the most important lessons you'll learn in this tracking business is that after you play, you have to pick up your toys."

"You call this play?" she said as she rubbed her arm.

I gave her a grin, "You grab the stakes. I'll grab the knives and arrows. Maybe we can see if Thomas will hide everything in his house in case we ever have to come back."

"I am never coming back here," informed Mindy.

"Sure, sis," I replied. "Me, too."

"What shall I collect?" asked Killian, following behind us like an eager puppy.

"I dunno," I said, looking around for some assignment. My eyes fell upon the motionless lumps of werepires and vampwolves we had left strewn about the street, "Would you mind taking care of those? We don't need any of them deciding what this town needs is to restock its ghosts."

"Come on, Killian," said Dad as he rested his hand on Killian's shoulder and steered him away, "Let me tell you about the time I stopped a horde of vampires at a homecoming bonfire..."

"Stay out of trouble!" Mom yelled.

By the time all of us were done, it was quiet as... well... the dead.

False dawn was starting to crest over the mountains. Mom had worked her magic and the ghosts were gone. We all looked like we were ready to fall over. Pretty much every inch of my body was bruised. I could have slept for a week. We had made it through the night, though, and that's what was important. It was also important not to spend another night here.

"All's-Well-That-Ends-with-the-Right-People-Dead-and-a-Paycheck, right Maggie?" joked my dad.

"We didn't get a paycheck for this job, Dad."

"Oh, now, listen to you, pessimistic pumpkin. I'm thinking we might get at least a couple months knocked off our rent. Who knows when Mr. Smith will be back? It's not safe to send off checks to an empty office. I'm thinking we might just hold off until he stops by personally to collect."

I smiled. I kind of hoped he did get away from Vaclav, just so Dad had an opportunity to make sure he received all his due.

"I'm so glad we were here to help those poor people," said Mom, sighing as she looked at the empty streets. "Can you imagine? Stuck out here for over a century."

"I can't imagine being stuck out here for another minute," Mindy replied. "Can we go yet?"

"Sounds fantastic!" I agreed.

Killian cleared his throat, "That could be problematic..."

I turned around to where he was looking. I had forgotten that our cars were now completely trashed thanks to Werewolf & Sons Junkyard Dogs.

"Shit."

Man, I was going to miss my car.

"Cars. We don't need no stinking cars," said Dad, throwing his arms around our shoulders. "Lucky for you guys, you have a couple of world walkers in the family."

"It was really wonderful to have a chance to get out here," said Mom, soaking in the last of Ghost Town. She paused, "You know, I was very surprised not to see Thomas try to cross over."

"Thomas said he wanted to stay here," said Mindy.

Mom stepped forward slowly, "Did you talk to Thomas? Did you actually hear him?"

"No. I meant... I..." Mindy stammered, wild eyed.

"My baby!" said Mom, running over to swoop her up in her arms and smother her with kisses all over her face. "I always knew it would be you."

"Help!" croaked Mindy.

I shrugged my shoulders, "Sorry. I have to open a portal. But we can come back to hang out with your imaginary friend anytime you'd like."

"I'm going to kill you, Maggie," she started to say, but was interrupted by more kissing and smothering.

I went over and gathered everyone up into a group hug, "What do you say we head home?"

I poked a little hole through the ether. Nothing came rushing at me. No lava, no fire, no saltwater, so I kept opening. I grabbed Killian and pushed him on through. Then grabbed Mindy and pushed her through. Then Mom and Dad and I followed behind, closing the door as I left.

Done and done.

Not bad for a night's work.

Chapter 27

Our portal opened up onto Main Street of Old Historic Orange. It's this restored town with brick sidewalks and adorable little thrift shops. I had forgotten how much I enjoyed things like intact glass windows and paved roads and living people.

The place was slowly starting to wake up. Loud delivery trucks were dropping off baked goods at the coffee shops and a couple of the antique showrooms already had their lights on.

"Oh, I always meant to come here," said Mom. "Funny how it takes leaving your dimension to get you to actually play tourist in a place you've lived your entire life."

Mindy and I rolled our eyes.

"Okay, kids, we need to find a ride up to Pasadena," Dad proclaimed, assessing one of the very real issues we had before us.

"Call home. Pipistrelle can come get us," said Mindy.

"Pipistrelle?" I asked. "Does he have his

license yet?"

Mindy shot me a look. She was done with our little family adventure.

I dialed my phone and the brownie's chirpy little voice came on the line. I had no idea what the cops were going to think about an infant-sized man driving a car down the 5 freeway. But this is Los Angeles, so I suppose they've seen weirder.

Mom suggested we browse in the antique shops and stop for a cup of coffee as we waited.

"I think we should start walking towards the freeway," said Mindy.

"That's not going to get us home to Pasadena any quicker," I pointed out.

She shot me a death glare, "We. Walk."

Mom stood there mystified, "Walk? No one walks in Los Angeles."

"We are in Orange County."

"It is the same rules."

"I don't think so, Mom," said Mindy.

Killian, sensing that perhaps this situation could use an elf's touch took my mom's elbow and suggested, "Think of it more as a leisurely stroll through the more historic parts of town."

So, we strolled. Through historic parts of town. Note to the world, I am not what one would call a particularly "good" window shopper. Unless it featured armament, in which case, I wasn't so

bad. I was about to crawl out of my fucking skin if I had to look at one more set of Fiestaware when the brownie finally decided to show up.

Dad, Mom, and Killian got into the back as Mindy buckled herself into the passenger seat, "Now, Pipistrelle, take us home!"

"Hold your horses," I said. I opened the door to the driver's side and hooked my finger, "Out. I'm driving."

"But I would be most honored to drive you to your destination," offered Pipistrelle.

"Listen, brownie, you're adorable and I'm sure that squeaky little voice of yours could talk your way out of any ticket, but I want someone behind the wheel who can see over the dashboard without a booster seat."

He gave me a little salute and climbed into the back, sliding into the seat belt with Killian.

"Sorry about the elbow room, Killian," I said.

He swung his arm around Pipistrelle and gave him a manly little jiggle hug, "It is always a pleasure to spend time in the presence of other fairy folk."

Pipistrelle looked up at him and beamed so big, I thought his face was going to crack and fall off.

They were soon deep into manly talk about midsummer parties and solstice plans as everyone

else tucked themselves in for forty winks.

I pulled up the car into the driveway and Pipistrelle popped out of the door before I had barely even stopped the vehicle. I swear to god that dumb little brownie was going to get himself killed if he didn't quit doing that.

Mom hopped out, arms spread wide as she announced, "We're finally here!"

As Mindy exited, she pointed a finger at all of us, "My husband is out of town. When he gets back, none of this ever happened. I was not on The Other Side. I did not stake a vampire. I did not hear a ghost. We never speak of this again."

Dad gave her a wink, "What happens in Ghost Town stays in Ghost Town."

Mindy nodded resolutely, glad it was settled. She skipped up the stairs and opened the door for Mom. I got out and leaned against the car, just glad to have a moment of quiet that wasn't fraught with something trying to make a meal out of us. Killian and Dad strolled over to join me.

Dad gave a great big sigh and stretched his arms over his head, "What a lovely morning."

"One of the best I've seen," I replied.

"You done good, kid," he said. "You, too, Killian. We showed those undead what's what."

"They're still out there," I said, a little sad that this moment was going to have to take a turn towards the more serious.

Dad nodded, "True. Vaclav is just a little more impenetrable. You still got that comb, Maggie?"

I pulled it out of my pocket as it gave me one last little jolt and dropped it on the ground, "Want to do the honors?"

He popped my trunk and pulled out my tire iron.

"This is for putting my baby girls under thrall," he said as he split the comb in two.

We stood there staring at the pieces. It was done.

"Guess we have to stock up our armory on more silver bullets. How many clips did you go through last night, Maggie?"

"A lot."

"Think you might be up for a shopping spree this afternoon?"

Sometimes having your enemies power up has its advantages.

"Next to gun metal black, silver is my favorite color," I said with a grin.

Dad gave me a hug and then yawned, "You know, I just don't know if I enjoy these all-nighters as much as I used to."

"You're telling me. I feel like I could sleep for a week."

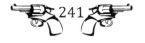

Dad got a little quiet and then said, "Your mom thinks I should consider hanging up my holster. What do you think about that?"

"That she's ridiculous."

"No, I'm serious, Maggie. What would you think about me retiring?"

I looked over at him, my heart dropping into my stomach, "What are you saying?"

"Maggie-girl, it's a shame that sometimes we just get old," he said, staring up at the morning sky. "I had a couple moments there where I realized I can't stake a vampire as well as I used to. After all that time I lost stuck in between dimensions and then last night... Just thinking maybe I'd like to make sure I'm around awhile longer and maybe a quieter lifestyle might help make that happen."

I nodded, feeling like someone had just poured ice water through my veins, "I don't know if I can do this without you, Dad."

"Sure you can," he said, planting a kiss on my head. "Sure you can."

He jammed his hands into his pockets and whistled his way up to Mindy's house. I stood there, watching him as he went, wondering what the heck I was going to do.

Killian cleared his throat.

"Oh, sorry Killian!" I said, rousing myself from the shock of my dad handing in his two

weeks notice. "I need to get you back to the elfin forest. Sorry. Um, as soon as I can get a car..."

He took my hand in his and gave it a gentle squeeze, "There is no rush."

I tried to give him a smile but I'm sure it came out a little more grimace-like than I had hoped, "Thanks for helping me to save the world. Again."

"All in a day's work," he said, looking up at the house, "So..."

"So."

We stood there.

"What will be your next course of action?" he asked.

I shook my head, "I have no idea..."

Except then, I had an idea and realized it had been standing there beside me the whole time, holding my sweaty palm in his cool hand.

"Killian," I began. I turned towards him, the words catching in my throat, "You've been here for me through all of this..."

I couldn't even look at him. I stared down at the ground, unable to finish the sentence.

He took my chin and gently tilted my face towards his, "Yes?"

"And I was wondering... if maybe..."

"Yes, Maggie?" he said, brushing back my hair.

We looked at one another, both knowing what I was about to say.

"Have you ever thought about becoming a professional tracker?" I asked.

"How is the pay?"

"Lousy," I said, "But I hear that the boss knows someone with a brownie who makes a kickass breakfast."

The smile spread across his face slowly. He wrapped me up in his big, strong arms and said, "I thought you would never ask."

Acknowledgements

I have been overwhelmed by the response to the *Maggie* series. You have no idea how much each kind review and fan letter has meant. I promise that more stories are on their way! I rely upon word of mouth, so if you liked this book, please tell your friends. And if you didn't, let's keep this book our little secret.

A very special thank you to Tammy Turk, Mary Stancavage, Tantris Hernandez, and Caitlin Bergendahl. Some of these women live close, one of lives far away, but over the years they have all been so unbelievably amazing in their support of me and my goofy dreams. Thank you. I'm so sorry you had to watch me in so many terrible shows.

Many thanks to my beta readers Caitlin Bergendahl, Adam Jackman, and Mia Winn for slogging through this mess. Oh boy, was it a mess... I owe you. A lot. And you all are BRILLIANT.

A special thanks to Mia & Ryan Winn and Erin Glaser for hosting me at more Comicons than I have any right to be at and allowing me to glom onto their awesomeness. Help me thank them, gentle readers, by checking out Sock Zombie, Giddy Girlie, and buying every single comic Ryan Winn inks. EVERY

SINGLE ONE! Gloms away!

This book was written as part of National Novel Writing Month. This year, I participated in a very special charity event for NaNoWriMo called The Night of Writing Dangerously. Two hundred and fifty authors descended upon the Julia Morgan Ballroom in downtown San Francisco dressed in our 1940s best. Armed only with our laptops (and typewriters. Some took the noir theme very seriously), we engaged in an evening of literary abandon, typing to our heart's content for six hours. I wrote the best parts of this book. The write-a-thon benefited the Young Writers Program, which funds free creative writing programs in hundreds of schools and communities around the world.

In order to get there, though, I needed some help. And that's where these fabulous folks came in. In alphabetical order, thank you to Caitlin Bergendahl, Bridget Franckowiak, Robin McWilliams & Madonna Cacciatore, Cassie Oates, Joe Purcell, Richard Van Slyke, Mary Stancavage, Ken Steadman, Ray Stilwell, Tammy Turk, and Christine & Tyler Wilhelm. This book, literally, would not have happened without you and there's a bunch of kids in needy schools who are thanking you, too.

Most of all, thank you always to my family, the best fan club a girl could ever want or need.

Maryland Distinguished Scholar in the Arts and twenty year veteran of stage and screen, Kate Danley received her B.S. in theatre from Towson University.

Her debut novel, *The Woodcutter*, was honored with the Garcia Award for the Best Fiction Book of the Year, named the 1st Place Fantasy Book in the Reader Views Literary Awards, and won the Sci-Fi/Fantasy category in the Next Generation Indie Book Awards.

Other titles include: *Maggie for Hire*, *Maggie Get Your Gun*, and *5:00 Breakout*.

Her plays have been produced in New York, Los Angeles, and Maryland. Her screenplay *Fairy Blood* won 1st Place in the Breckenridge Festival of Film Screenwriting Competition in the Action/Adventure Category and her screenplay *American Privateer* was a 2nd Round Choice in the Carl Sautter Memorial Screenwriting Competition.

Her films and shorts *The Playhouse*, *Dog Days*, *Sock Zombie*, *SuperPout*, and *Sports Scents* can be seen in festivals and on the internet.

She lost on Hollywood Squares.

For more info visit www.katedanley.com

Also by Kate Danley

Winner of the Garcia Award for
Best Fiction Book of the Year

1st Place Fantasy Book
Reader Views Reviewers Choice Awards

Winner of the Sci-Fi/Fantasy Category
Indie Book Awards

Available in Paperback & e-Book

Maggie MacKay
Magical Tracker Series

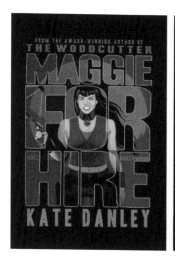 

"If urban fantasy could be bottled, then this story is a shot-glass full of awesomesauce."
- Dark Side of the Covers

Maggie for Hire
Maggie Get Your Gun

Book Three Coming in 2013!

FROM THE AWARD WINNING AUTHOR OF
THE WOODCUTTER

5800

BREAKOUT

KATE DANLEY

A short story about having to escape
the office...

Available exclusively on Kindle and
Nook.